The Fairy Tales of London Town

VOLUME ONE

Upon Paul's Steeple

Other titles by William Mayne published by
Hodder Children's Books

Earthfasts
Cradlefasts

The Fairy Tales of London Town

VOLUME ONE
Upon Paul's Steeple

William Mayne

Hodder
Children's
Books

A division of Hodder Headline plc

Published by Hodder Children's Books 1995

10 9 8 7 6 5 4 3 2 1

ISBN 0 340 64858 9

Printed and bound in Great Britain by
Mackays of Chatham PLC, Chatham, Kent

Hodder Children's Books
A division of Hodder Headline plc
338 Euston Road
London NW1 3BH

For
Winifred,
beloved aunt,
whose mother as a child
played upon the steps
of
Saint Paul's Cathedral

⊗ Contents ⊗

Upon Paul's Steeple

Upon Paul's steeple stands a tree
As full of fruit as it may be;
   The little boys of London Town,
They run with hooks to pull them down;
   And then they go from hedge to hedge
Until they come to London Bridge.

Strandhoggers

Fairies avoid people most of the time. But sometimes they have to mix, and they can do it in quite a rough way

For instance, if you offend them they will beat you, quite badly if you meant to harm them.

On the other hand, if they want something they will take it, and if you resist you will at least be pinched, and probably bruised as well.

There have always been Strandhoggers. They are an ordinary affliction of the human race, called raiding and piracy. But it's odd to see fairies being Strandhoggers.

And nobody will believe you if you say so. Except once, if you were there, they sometimes will, because it was in the paper. And this time it was done by persuasion, and hardly anybody was pinched, bruised, or offended. Though there is a long-serving police officer with an embarrassing affliction.

There is a piece of London that once was a pleasant beach, full of sand and lying in the sun. Once a clean river washed against it, and the new tide each day. Now the river is narrow and dirty and there is no beach, only houses looking the other way.

The place was called the Strand, meaning the edge of the water and it still is. But in 1953, and probably for ever, it was a street with big offices along both sides, hotels, theatres, colleges, shops, and traffic on black tarmac.

No one would think fairies would come there for any reason. No one would think they would do what they did. We may not like it, but they play by their rules, not ours. Not that Strandhogging isn't one of our pleasures.

It was a sunny day in May, 1953, but with a nippy little breeze from the east, so that people put on a raincoat for warmth, and the buses had their heaters on.

Kathryn Browne was on a bus going towards Aldwych about midday, going to work for the BBC World Service, where she read things out for the listeners in foreign lands. Today a foreign land was coming to her.

Apparently they listen to broadcasts in Fairyland as well as in this world, because a young prince of Elfhame, named Alenzir, had heard her voice and fallen very badly in love with her. This was virtually before television, too.

Kathryn was not in love with anyone, but was only very fond of her cat and a white rabbit she had had since she was twelve. They stayed at home with her old aunty, so she was alone on the bus, like the rest of the passengers. She had really felt alone ever since her parents died in an air raid when she was seven, ten years before.

The bus stopped in the middle of the road, where the traffic suddenly jammed itself. That happens in London. Along the Strand at that time buildings were being rebuilt, and wagons were often backing into sites, or coming out.

People looked out of the bus, and their heads all shook when the bus started again and then stopped once again, suddenly.

This time the driver leaned out and shouted at someone. Then when he started again the engine stalled with a jerk, and nothing happened.

Kathryn thought she would get out and walk, not wanting to be late for work.

But she first looked out of the window, straight ahead, to be sure it was not too far. She saw why the bus had stopped and become uncertain.

But she took no notice. She knew that there was a road ahead, full of traffic. She knew she could not see what her eyes told her about.

She told herself it was a reflection. The woman sitting next to her said it looked just like a fleet of ships sailing across the road and pushing up on to a beach.

Kathryn saw their strange square sails drop down.

"It's a reflection," she told the woman. "It just looks as if it's there."

"So do things that are there," said the woman.

"That's why we get confused," said Kathryn, because she was a sensible girl, and knew that what she saw wasn't really there, of course. Neither of them wanted to say what they saw or what they thought, in case of being thought funny in some way.

You don't want to be carried away mad as a hatter in front of the BBC World Service.

You don't want to be carried away at all.

"It's the glass that's dirty," said Kathryn.

She certainly wasn't considering being carried away by

anything stranger than a bus. And this one was failing her.

So she got off the stationary vehicle. The ground was ankle-deep in water. The hard black road was not truly there, only golden sand under the water.

Kathryn was not wet, but she tiptoed to the pavement. No traffic was moving, so she was not run over.

However, a boat sailed straight past the bus alongside her, and beached itself. She had to step aside smartly, avoiding a starfish, or the top bar of the sail would have fallen on her when the crew ran it down.

She had been riding in a real bus, smelling of dust and smoke and fuel oil. But now the ship was more real, and the bus had gone thin and shadowy.

"Nonsense," said Kathryn to herself, and thought the bus back into being solid once more, and the ship into being part of a dream. It was like forcing an optical illusion not to mislead. "I shall wake up."

Not far ahead, on the pavement, or a sand-dune, people were becoming excited. There was a fight starting, and voices were calling for the police and the army, and saying there was an invasion.

Invasions often start with ships on the beach and men jumping out of them, and that was what people saw now. Some of those people had been soldiers until a few years ago, and they knew they had to fight, even if they only had their fists.

Some people believed what they saw round them, and others didn't. The believers fell over the ships and into the water. The non-believers knew there was no water and refused to see the ships and fell over bicycles and carts instead. Many of either sort thought their fellow citizens had gone mad and were about to execute them with their umbrellas.

Others saw something but didn't know what it was. A crowd gathered by Kathryn's bus, thinking that it had run over a cart full of dancers.

"Ah," said Kathryn, "it is a dream. There is nothing to worry about." In real life dancers do not go about in carts.

There was a policeman now, who had got hold of somebody and was telling him to keep still, my lad. But the arrested person was going in and out of reality, sometimes fading, sometimes distinct, and the policeman was moving his head from side to side and up and down to get a proper focus on him.

"Now you stop that," he said. "That won't do you no good."

But matters began to change. The Londoners were getting annoyed now, and not frightened of invaders but of something else. It was irritating to have strangers walking right through you, yet it was soon over, but to have the same strangers actually standing where you were, almost in your own shoes, was too much, and didn't feel quite decent.

There was little they could do about it. You can't hit a person who occupies the same space or you hit yourself. But it is very unnerving while it is happening, and now, forty years on, not everyone has recovered. "After all," said one old gentleman to me last week, "you can't be sure who has been shaved; and if it's his tummy-ache I don't deserve it. Also, who is in charge of thinking? But at least, if there's anyone there, he doesn't cost much."

Kathryn was thinking that when she was little she would have known that these people were . . .

The dancers were being brought out from under the bus. They were not in the least hurt, or run over. Their boat had simply parked there. They were not necessarily dancers, but the mistake was natural, because they wore such pretty clothes of such fine material.

Except that these were not clothes, but wings.

Angels, Kathryn thought. I am dead. Who will look after Pussy and Bunny?

But angels have luxurious wings of a feathery white kind, and these wings were silken and coloured so bright.

So Kathryn knew. Why couldn't I see them when I believed in them? she wondered. It's not fair to do it now when I don't.

And to make sure she did not believe she turned up towards Southampton Street to go through back ways to Bush House.

She couldn't even get there just then, because so many people were all round her. Luckily no one was jostling her, or walking through her, or indeed bothering her at all.

Then some of those there were lining up on the sand and lifting up long golden trumpets.

"It *is* angels," said Kathryn. "I suppose I believe in them more than I do in fairies, but not much. And I know which I'd rather have."

The trumpets sounded. Angels are sure to sound one unmistakable way. You would know it when you heard it, and it would make you shiver. But this was faraway fairy music, shimmering, not shouting, exciting and not challenging, romantic and not asking about your sins and your soul. Comforting and thrilling and other-worldly, inviting without asking whether you have been good enough to enter here.

The policeman took off his helmet and rubbed his face. He was not going to believe this stuff while on duty. "Now, then," he was saying.

But everybody, man, woman, or fairy, turned on him and shut him up.

The trumpeters stepped back smartly, and Kathryn, because she was straight in line with them, saw a clear space in front of them.

Into the space drove a larger ship, golden and high, with sails like flowers, masts like green reeds, and flags like all the stars of the sky, and the sun in some of them too.

The sail came down sharp. Over the side stepped a fairy man, dressed like a prince, putting his foot in the tide but not getting wet.

The trumpets sounded again, all pointing towards the land and to Kathryn.

I am in the way, she thought. Where shall I go?

She did not know where she was going, and didn't make it. Her legs simply did nothing but stand there. The fairy prince walked through the water on to dry beach, took off his cap, fluttered his wings in a polite way, and dropped to his knees.

He's fallen over, Kathryn thought. Poor thing. He is so slender and not at all strong.

He was kneeling on purpose, on a tussock of grass, where most people would have seen only the kerb of the road. Now there were flowers growing in it.

"Lady," he said, "I have come all the way from Elfhame, and cannot return without you."

"Yes, you can," said Kathryn, not hearing him quite clearly because his voice was so soft. "It's on the North

Kent line from London Bridge." She thought he had said Eltham.

"Never," he said. "I am Alenzir, Prince of Elfhame, and your voice has haunted my dreams, and what you say is so wise I am enchanted by every word."

"I just read out what they tell me," said Kathryn, who sometimes found it all a very great bore and wondered if publishing wouldn't be a better career.

She was trying to get away now, because Alenzir was stretching out his hands to hold hers if he could, and lifting himself a little with his wings, but there were still people behind her.

"Is this gent bothering you, miss?" asked the policeman.

Prince Alenzir looked at him, flicked a finger, and the policeman hopped away as a toad. He recovered after half a dozen jumps, but when he approached again he turned into a toad. So he had a choice, and stayed a policeman.

"I shall be late for work," said Kathryn.

"Work?" said the prince. "What is that?"

"I think publishing might be better," said Kathryn. "And safer."

"Please speak again," said the prince. "Tell me about the expedition to Mount Everest. Tell me once more about the tonnage of wheat in Alberta, Canada, because even when I do not understand your words I still love your voice."

In the end there is nothing much you can do about the fairy folk. They have a hundred ways of taking you if they want you, and as many ways of keeping you once they have taken you.

Now and then you make a decision that changes your life. Kathryn made one just then. "Just go to my aunty's house in Bayswater," she said, "and bring my cat and my rabbit, and I'll go with you."

Prince Alenzir lifted her up in his arms, spread his wings, and carried her to his boat.

All the boats departed, the sands went away, the road reappeared, and the houses, theatres, museums and shops reappeared. Some of it was in the paper, but there was so much detail no one ever understood the event at all.

Kathryn is in Elfhame still, taken in broad daylight in a London street. Some say she thought she was going to Kent, but who would want to do that, even from London Bridge? A quiet girl, she seemed to have taken Pussy and Bunny with her, her aunt said, in Bayswater.

The policeman has given a lot of evidence about one thing and another, but when he gets excited no one believes a toad.

ᴄᴏ *The Willing Pupil* ᴄᴏ

There was a school once in Clerkenwell belonging to St John's church, so the schoolmaster was the parson there, and his name was Dr Frobisher, and the school was for boys because he could not abide little girls.

Mind you, the pupils thought he could not abide boys either, for they were switched daily with his ferule, and they were glad to get out at the end of the day and show each other their bruises and cuts.

Said Dr Frobisher, that it brought them out of idleness and folly to be good clerks at least, and if one of them in a hundred years became a doctor of divine studies, then all the bruises and hurts were worth it, because of all people a Doctor of Divinity had a front seat in the world to come.

He might be right, and he might be wrong. Wrong, said the boys, it was Hell for him, a seat right on the bars. But we don't know, they might say it for spite.

Because boys do not like to work, but if they don't work when they are young they never will, as you can tell.

But some try harder than others, and if they are less bright in their wits they might try over-much.

So it was with Tom Dresser. He was a frail boy in any case, but one who wanted to get on, one who studied his books, wrote his best, and was never at the root of mischief but sat back and kept quiet.

For all that he got his share of beating, because the Doctor said that he must be misbehaving in secret somehow, because misconduct is natural in boys.

But poor Tom would sit his lessons out, and lift a thin arm to beg the meaning of this and that as they went through their Latin, Hickory Dickory Dock, or their Rules of Practice or the Kings of Judah.

Tom would despair of keeping them in his mind, write them in his books as he might, his nib forever dipping and scribing and the words flowing in a neat hand that all the other louts envied. So much did they think it unnatural that they would often scribble over what he had written and spoil the work so that he had it to do again. And of course be beaten for what was spoiled.

He would take his work home, in a woven strap, and then instead of playing along the street would sit by the window and con his book. It was his aim to gain a good position as a clerk and maintain his mother, who had cared for him these last twelve years.

But, do what he would, in the end of some of the days a sort of faintness would come over him, and he would lean back on his stool against the wall and feel waves of darkness passing through his head.

Most of us would think Tom needed sleep, but it was not quite that.

After a time he would seem to be in another place, without having slept. He would come into a silvery world where all was quiet, and be sitting under a tree, at peace with all the world.

Then he would wake at his table at home, and set to his work again. It was as good as a night's rest, he told his mother, the first few times that happened to him. He sat and saw the gentle landscape going off into mist, he told his mother, and in that place he would hear music and think that someone was dancing, and before knowing it he would be asleep there. And then he was at home at the table.

But she thought he had only blinked and yawned, as well he might.

After some days when this happened (not every week) he began to see more of the other place. He saw he was sitting on fresh green grass, and that not far off there were quaint little houses, almost as if they were made of bread, he told his mother. And he almost brought back the tunes of music that he heard, but wondered what instrument they were played on.

I will sleep when I am a man, Tom told his mother. That will not be long.

Then instead of visiting that place about once a week, he began to be taken there every night, and for longer times. His mother would find him sprawled on the floor where he had fallen, and she could not wake him.

Tom was frail to begin with, but now he did not eat well, and became a bundle of bones. But he worked as hard as ever. So little was there of him that Dr Frobisher could no longer bring himself to lay the stick across his shoulders, in case, he said, he broke the stick.

But he might have known what was to come. Solemnly he told all the boys to be ready for the next world. They joked about that and said that the world they wanted put money in their pockets and strong ale in their bellies. But they did not say it to Dr Frobisher.

Now, every night of the winter, Tom was astray in the other world. He heard the music still, and he began to see the people, queer and strange, he told his mother, like thin babies walking and talking, grown or small, not a stitch on them, man, woman, or child.

Oh hush, said his mother.

Sometimes they were dancing. At other times they sat and ate their food. Often they came up and looked into his eyes, and sometimes the young ones would feel at his elbow or slap his foot.

He was not there when he was not there, Tom said. When he found himself in that place they looked and noticed that he had arrived. They did not know yet what to make of him. He did not know what to make of them.

But at last they waited for him, and were glad to see him. He began to hear their voices.

They are teaching me, he told his mother. All that I have learned and forgotten comes to me again and I know and remember it. It is all in the music.

However it was, from then on he recalled all that he was taught, and Dr Frobisher began to be amazed.

You will be no mere tally clerk in counting house, he told Tom, but go on to the schools at Oxford and be greatly learned. But Tom told him nothing, for after all, his visiting took place when he was at home.

And then, one day, it came to him in his lessons. The other boys saw him sitting against the wall and staring. But before they made Dr Frobisher see him, and lay the stick across him for insolence and idleness, he woke again, smiled (because some lesson had come clear to his mind), and wrote what the strange little people had told him.

But the boy next to him wished to know what the music was. Tom could not tell him.

Dr Frobisher told that boy to let Tom Dresser alone and do his own work.

Often and often, as the spring approached, Tom went into that dwam, and to save him, because boys are full of kindly feeling if they are let alone, the other pupils would gently shake his shoulder to keep the punishing stick from him, even if it brought it upon them instead.

They teased Tom no more. They took him now as their lucky charm, what they call in the north a mascot, and would carry his books for him, or bring him half a penny bun, or ask his opinion on this and that.

They are very kind, Tom told his mother. But she could say nothing, nor be more kind, though she saw that Tom was on his way to some other world, known or not.

And so it came about. One day in school he leaned on the wall, and would have fallen, if the boy next to him and the boy behind had not suppported him. Tom was away in that other land, and this time he was not being given a lesson there, but given something else. And there was music sounding in the dark schoolroom.

The other boys were alarmed now, to see him holding a deep stare. This was more than happened before, and he did not wake. One of them ran to Tom's mother's house to bring her along. He was beaten for this when he came back in. But following him came Tom's mother.

When he saw her, Dr Frobisher left off that boy and turned to Tom, who was sitting stiff and open-eyed.

What is this, sir? he asked, wanting to be seen as the good teacher in front of the mother. He up with his rod and touched Tom's shoulder, and Tom woke a little.

Tom moved his eyes, smiled to his mother, and looked humbly at Dr Frobisher.

They have, he said, such bread in that place, and began to write in his book. I have tasted it.

And that was it. Perhaps he went to that calm world of music where the little people were on the neat grass. Perhaps he went elsewhere. He will not meet Dr Frobisher.

So the other boys carried him to his home and laid him on his bed. Dr Frobisher did not see them again that day. But he was changed by what had happened, in case he had killed his best pupil in front of the mother.

The next time they were together he wept before the class, and broke up the rod, and never again did he touch them with it.

And this happened not because Tom was dead to this world, but because his book, lying on his desk with the wet pen on it, was not finished.

As they watched, for the next six or seven days, and while they did not dare touch, the words of the lessons were being inscribed line after line in a writing that was Tom's, but by no human hand.

∽ *Whip Away* ∽

Up at Piccadilly-O
The coachman takes his stand,
   And when he spies a pretty girl
He takes her by the hand –
   Whip-away for ever-O,
Drive away so clever-O,
   All the way to Taunton-O
He drives her four-in-hand.

∞ *The Bascule* ∞

Like other bridges in the land, Tower Bridge has its own other-worldly inhabitant, a familiar. The Tower Bridge familiar is now a strong and hairy goblin known as the Bascule, or some name like it, depending on your point of view and manners.

He is reputed not to be the first to live in the bridge. When it was first built something a little more friendly installed itself.

There were some complaints even about that, because the bridge was built by Act of Parliament, and no mention was made of such an infestation.

But then, no mention was made of rats, which live there too, or swallows.

However, the bridge came to be dreaded by a series of supernatural beings. A bridge-creature's duty is to keep the bridge, and it is understood this means that the bridge has to cross right over the river all of the time. When the bridgemaster keeps opening the middle to let ships through, the first spirits either felt they had failed, or were outright killed by the moving parts.

Men did not understand this very well, and thought nothing of it. But without a guardian of some sort things will go wrong, like the cart that jammed across the lifting deck in 1897 and had to be dismantled by steeplejacks. The horse was found in Holland eight days later, its shoes very rusty from seawater, and not understanding foreign traffic.

The Act of Parliament says the bridge has to open for ships, even quite small ones. None of them must be kept waiting.

The matter was a problem for all guardians who wanted to keep a fine bridge. Some left under the stress, and took over pedestrian overpasses. One who can't keep his or her bridge suffers a breakdown and nervous collapse of his or her own. These poor creatures had to take the most menial jobs, supervising stiles and gratings, hardly ever noticed, and badly underpaid. Though gratings often produce lost coins and car keys, as well as dirty water from road edges.

Bridgemasters know about their guardians, and keep them sweet with small accidental gifts like milk or paint of a pretty colour – a good guardian will sometimes touch up the bits men can't easily get at.

A succession of lady guardians, all attracted by the pretty aspect of the bridge, tried their hand. There is no record of what happened to them all, but two were later known to be managing a set of trestle tables at Smithfield – a horrid dirty job when lambs were chopped up on the tables.

Then some males tried their hands, attracted by the mechanical parts of the bridge. They did not understand what the mechanical parts were for, and one after the other had to go to the Herbal Garden for remedies, and look for lighter work.

The position lay empty for a time. This was when rust got in under the roadway. But then there came the Bascule, who had been running a heavy-duty railway viaduct in the north until it was pulled down. He was very experienced: his viaduct actually had sets of points on it and semaphore signals to play with – the Bascule had no sympathy with fluttery things like that.

With his compensation money, which he got after a big struggle on his behalf by his union (the Lares and Penates), the Bascule came to London, hoping really for some appointment on the Westway.

But he was fascinated by Tower Bridge, and looked upon it as a challenge.

The bridgemaster learnt fairly soon that the new guardian did not want saucers of milk, thank you, but a good chunk of raw beef and a bottle of Newcastle Brown.

And he really is very strong, and very aware of dangers. There are times when the bridge cannot be opened. The machinery can't hack it. At those times the bridgemaster has to go out to the middle of the lifting deck and talk to the Bascule.

There the Bascule is engaged on his constant pastime, which he calls rayballing. It is more than a pastime, in fact; it is part of his duty.

Down in the Thames is the young serpent. Serpents breed in fresh water, like salmon. This one has not yet left the Thames for the high seas, but when it does it will pass under Tower Bridge. After a good many years more it will return to breed, with its mate. Between them they will tear down even Tower Bridge, open or not.

That danger the Bascule must avert. So he hangs a sock on a line down in the water, and sits in the middle of the bridge when the tide is right, waiting for the young serpent to bite. (Other rayballers have to fill their socks with worms, but the Bascule is powerful enough not to need them.)

Since the middle is where the bridge opens there is often a conflict. The Bascule is strong enough to hold the bridge shut, and that is what he does.

That is his duty in any case. Sometimes he does allow the bridge to open – every living creature, even a cheese, has a right to yawn, and that, he thinks, is what the bridge is doing.

But at rayballing time nothing will shift him.

Parliament has not thought much about the matter, as usual; and if it does that will not move the Bascule. Ships will have to wait. The Bascule is not giving up his job for anyone else's convenience.

If you see him rayballing you will have to stop, whether the bridge is open or not. Don't disturb him. His duty is to the bridge, not to you.

Or go round by Chelsea, which is kept by a very gentle lady guardian, who appreciates honey sandwiches.

The Cock Lane Ghost

Unusual hauntings in Cock Lane, in the City, were the talk of the town in 1762. In those days people had little understanding of ghosts, and people who ought to have been more sensible became excited, and inconsiderate. Ghosts, after all, have a right to be ghosts, and if we hear them or see them we should pay attention quietly. Someone is trying to tell us something. That someone might be dead, or might be alive, or might be somewhere between. With the Cock Lane ghost we cannot be sure.

Some years before the trouble began a man in Norfolk, William Kent, lost his wife. She died, and that broke him up. He fell in love with the dead wife's sister, Fanny, and went to find whether he could marry her.

But the law then was that he couldn't, and they told him so. You can now, if you are a man, but you couldn't then. And she had kept house for him during his wife's illness, and was still there, so he saw her every day, and the law of the land said he could not have her as his next wife.

He left and came to London. He took lodgings with William Parsons, who was clerk of St Sepulchre's Church, Holborn. He was broken-hearted twice, once for losing his wife, and once for not being able to marry Fanny. Also he was made to feel guilty because he wanted to marry Fanny. These are strong feelings.

Whether he sent for Fanny, or whether she found him, we don't know. But she loved him, and perhaps she just came. Then they thought, no one knows us, so why should we not say we happen to be married, and who's to know? So he called her Mrs Kent, and she called him My Love.

They didn't know that they would feel even more guilty, because it was the rule then to be married if you said you were. So all the feelings grew stronger.

One night William Kent had to be away. No one knows what his work was, but some think he was a cobbler and bootmaker, and maybe he had gone to buy leather.

Fanny was nervous about being at home alone with just a candle, and they hadn't been able to keep a cat. She asked Mr Parsons' daughter Elizabeth to keep her company that night and sleep in the small bed.

But no one slept, because that night the noises started. Fanny was frightened before they began, and grew more and more terrified at the thuds and hollow clicks, the rattling and groanings, the rapping, scraping and scratching that filled the room.

Poor little Elizabeth fared no better. Fanny was telling her all the time that these noises were to tell her that she (Fanny) would die, because that is one of the ways omens come in Norfolk. And while the room grew quieter, it was only so that some invisible thing could walk through and turn the air cold and make the hair on their heads rise.

When William Kent came back and heard all this he moved Fanny away to Clerkenwell, where Fanny unhappily died like her sister, but of smallpox.

William Parsons, the landlord, and William Kent, and no doubt Elizabeth, thought that was the end of the matter.

But a year and a half later the noises began again in Cock Lane. The ghost of poor Fanny was blamed for it all, and so was a cobbler next door that William Kent had worked for. Elizabeth could actually see it on occasions. Apparently it looked just like a ghost, luminous and wandering; so it must have been there.

It wandered in and out of neighbouring houses up and down Cock Lane, whether the people believed in it or not. They grew very tired of it.

At last they complained, and the council sent round a clergyman, Stephen Aldrich, to bust it. He had the help of a Miss Fraser, who sometimes baby-sat Elizabeth. They decided to hold a séance and hack into the ghost circuits.

They managed to do that, and held conversations with Fanny. The conversations were slow, with Fanny answering one knock for 'Yes', two for 'No'.

"Yes," she said, when they asked whether she was Fanny. Then she told them she had not died of smallpox at all, but had been poisoned by William Kent, and was going to haunt the world until he was hanged for murder.

That was news, if you believed it. Newspapers were the same then as they are now. If there had been photographers you wouldn't have been able to get along Cock Lane for tripods and camera rostrums.

It was then that famous people came to listen. No doubt Miss Fraser tried to sell her story for money. She must have been annoyed that film rights hadn't been invented. Learned doctors asked questions, royal dukes came to peer. Poets wrote rotten poetry. The Cock Lane ghost was the talk of the town, and well known throughout the country.

"Cock Lane latest," the newspapers said. "New exclusive interview," and so on. "Hauntings terrify neighbourhood. What is the government going to do?"

Sometimes things don't go according to plan. Perhaps the ghost was frightened off, and wasn't there when Miss Fraser, and Elizabeth, thought it would be, to answer more questions.

At any rate, Elizabeth began to help a bit more than she should. They found her lying in her bed, listening to what was being said beyond the wall, and rapping on the wall with a stick like a drumstick. Making a fair noise, and adding bits that Fanny hadn't even begun to discuss.

Well, what do people expect, coming in mob-handed on a shy creature like a ghost, with a good story to tell? Elizabeth was trying to help someone really present but unable to speak in her own voice.

All at once the world preferred to believe it had been cheated all the time. No one after that tried to help poor Fanny. And no one tried to help William Kent. Would you be able to believe a ghost who might happen to be a little girl with a knee that clicked loudly when she wanted it to?

Her father, Mr Parsons, had to stand in the pillory, arms and head locked through a sort of board so that people could jeer at him and throw old cabbages. His family, Mr Aldritch, and Miss Fraser, were taken to the police court and charged with getting together to cheat.

It was not fair on William Kent. People went on believing what the ghost said after they didn't believe there had been one. They always looked sideways at him, and he probably went back to Norfolk.

But there was one good thing for William Parsons, because the people took up a collection for him. Perhaps poor Elizabeth was now blamed for everything.

Not many people, to this day, walk up and down Cock Lane at night. That's the ghost, not a helpful little girl.

But like most ghost stories, you can't believe the ghost and you can't believe the explanation. That's the haunting thing.

❧ *Nancy* ❧

Comes the day Nancy he living in the block of flats in the Isle of Dogs, long time since he travel there in the bananas and get chased out of a shop, now he pay all tax and get benefit but you know always the rain come down and the ships don't come no more and he can't get home.

Silly thing, he say just to himself and don't want nobody hearing, silly thing to sleep in that hand of bananas and get travelling here. But don't deserve it dark all day and no trees down in London, not a mango, not a banana, not a coconut, not a breadfruit.

He get letters from home, oh the weather, they say, just all this damn eternal sunshine praise the Lord and the hurricane, wooh!

But Nancy he get trouble going down to fetch these letters, way down the stairs round and round, bad enough, way up again, round and round, no way, man, that can suit him. Well, he so fat and puffed out, and legs tired, he got so many and now it feel he grow some more!

Now Snake living on the roof there in the pipes and all the gutters and the view, he say, like a telescope peeping, he can look in the girl windows, they don't know. Snake come up and down them stairs like a train, no trouble to him, Snake coming up there when Nancy on the way down and all the trouble of that, Snake bringing up his own birthday card.

Many happy weturns for you, Snake, say Nancy, he can't say his letters right, but not many happy weturns for Nancy. All the way up and not got twaction like you, man, say Nancy. There ain't no one like you for bwinging letters along, Snake, so maybe you help Nancy with impediment in his walk, and you got the kindest heart in all the world.

Snake put down his card. He like being thought nice fellow. Of course I help Nancy, he tell Nancy. Nancy, you hold my card and I look for his letter.

So he turn round, so easy, on the stair, and go for Nancy's letter.

When he come back Nancy say, Why, you gone so soon then, I forget to say the newspaper there too.

No trouble, Snake say, and down and up again he go.

When he get back Nancy say, Well, how if you do that each day for poor old Nancy so far woff his home, has to hear fwom his folks in the sunshine. And maybe fetch Nancy poor little bits shopping by times.

If you paying something, Snake say.

Oh, that easy, say Nancy. Snake, I know you like taste of blood, you like that vewy well. So you come in my flat each night and take a bite at my head, just a little bite, and you get my letters for me.

I do that, say Snake. Yes, I do that. That a neighbourly arrangement, man, so right on. And they shake hands on that, it no trouble.

Next day Snake there at Nancy door to get that work done first off and earn his bite at Nancy.

I like newspaper first, say Nancy. And in a bit of time after wit my letter.

So that come to two times up and down. And then Nancy want a yam out of the shop. Then he want some bones from the butcher and make soup. And then Nancy write a letter and Snake post that in the High Street, and work all day for Snake wearing out the tread of his new skin. But Snake looking forward to blood that night, and biting Nancy's head, so he work on.

And that night Nancy stand by his pay, and Snake come in at the door and bite Nancy on the head and got his blood.

But that not very good to Nancy, so he want two things, Snake to go on working, and Nancy not to pay any more, he don't stand another bite like that, wooh, it hurt!

Nancy think about that all next day, and Snake he begin to wonder too, up and down them steps and out along the street in daytime getting trod on, and no time to look through telescope at girls. And extra more work too, because Nancy invite White Rabbit from flat in basement.

White Rabbit the keeper of the cleaner, but glad to visit Nancy and get a dinner. He say, You don't get good service these days from such as cleaner, but this best carrot stew for weeks and if that black pot empty, well I done the best I could.

All good time for you, man, say Nancy. But that black iron pot fully empty. So now you go to bed, take pillow and quilt and bed and I sleep on kitchen floor.

The White Rabbit wonder why Nancy go to sleep on floor, and White Rabbit get the bed. No, say Rabbit, don't do that. I will sleep on kitchen floor, you keep your own proper bed.

Oh no, White Wabbit, say Nancy, I am not hearing that. I sleep on kitchen floor, and you take pillow and quilt and you sleep like Queen.

Then it all dark. But White Rabbit more used to straw than pillow and quilt, and don't trust Nancy all the way to Kingston. He know too from the cleaner where all the ways go in this block of flats, so down he go through the rubbish hole and into his own flat in basement and sleep there.

Snake come along to Nancy's door. Nancy, Nancy, don't you forget, here Snake come for his pay.

But White Rabbit not there to open door, not there at all. Nancy get up from floor and go to bedroom. Wabbit, he say, the door your side of house, you open door to neighbour. Wabbit, you hear!

And Snake outside shouting for Nancy to get door open and pay up. Take you in the court, Nancy and judge give me my pay.

Well, Nancy can't stand that, think Nancy. But he don't know why White Rabbit so quiet, till he go in room and find pillow on floor and quilt by wall, and something been down the rubbish chute and no White Rabbit in the place.

That Wabbit go down any hole, say Nancy. So he call to Snake, Oh, that bite hurt so much, I been to hospital, the doctor say another bite kill me.

The first bite always just the worst, say Snake. Next one only half, and the third, why, you never notice.

I be dead by then, think Nancy. And if I get a fourth, why then I not even have a ghost. So what can Nancy do?

Then he understand. He put on his head that big black iron pot where White Rabbit finish all the carrot stew. Now come in, Snake, he call. I just dreaming, sorry man, come in, I ready for you.

And I ready for you, says Snake, all up and poison now is Snake, and he remember you don't trust Nancy unless you foolish. He strike hard at Nancy's head, and he break a tooth, and he strike again and by God he break another tooth, and then he give up and go to the hospital and tell them Nancy done it.

What you put on his head to do this? he ask.

Never see Nancy, they say at the hospital. Wooh! Don't want to see Nancy.

That's it, man, say Snake, we don't never want to see Nancy.

And he went on home all bandage and taking snake aspirin, and give up the job of postman to Nancy, and spend the day telescoping at the girls but he can't smile at none until his smile grow back.

Nancy, he no better still, and got too much smile all the time.

⚈ *The Cat with Her Kits* ⚈

Russian soldiers with snow on their boots came marching through the country about a hundred years ago. The government said it wasn't true, but plenty of people saw them, and how else would they know? The soldiers were all just simple lads got lost, thinking they were in Poland or Belgium, one of those places.

This is true and it happened to my uncle Percy, and you can depend on him, he was a keeper at the zoo in London and I've been at his house when he took animals home so I've seen monkeys looking in mirrors and black pigs asleep on the hearth-rug, so I know this story is just right.

He'd let squirrels into his house, which was by the canal in a little woodland garden. That's how the soldiers came to his house, it was like theirs at home and they thought it might be friendly. The government was catching them and chaining them up and putting them in the prison before making them walk back to Russia and it was still winter.

So my uncle Percy was very soft and let three of them in. "Just mind the cat," he said, because he had a little lion home for the weekend, but the lion was shy and got behind the chair so it wasn't a problem. Uncle Percy didn't want them to tease it.

Off he went to get them a cup of tea and a sandwich,

because he could tell it was like feeding time.

Then it was just like hitch-hikers, I suppose, because, when his back was turned, not just three Russian lads came in, but those first ones held the door open and it was four, five, six, and I don't know how many more, but a houseful.

So he just put the kettle on again, because if the first three were needing help, so were the rest, far from their own country and people, like the animals in the zoo.

He doesn't think they were stealing, but by and by they weren't drinking tea but beer out of his barrel. And then they were frying his bacon in great thick slices and boiling his potatoes. Then they were into the puddings and the brandy and it was a Russian party, Uncle Percy thought.

And all the time the little lion was behind the chair keeping out of the way, but he got his tail trodden on and growled a bit.

Now, one of the lads, a corporal with stripes, was toasting a sausage on the fire and he liked it hard done so it was black and flames spurting out.

"Well, puss," he said, "would you like your tea now?" and he put this hot flaming sausage out to the lion, and the other lads weren't thinking but cheering him on.

The lion had had enough of them by now, getting trodden on and his whiskers singed, so he got up from behind the chair and slapped one or two, and cussed a bit, and roared, and got in a bite on a backside here and there, until all the Russian soldiers jumped out of the windows and left London.

Uncle Percy had to sort out the mess, and it was a pretty fair pigsty, and snow everywhere too, which is how you can tell it's a real true story, he wouldn't make that up.

And on Monday he went back to work. He didn't rightly know what happened to the soldiers, but he thought the government caught them all and sent them back, and that might be best, and then he forgot them.

But not long since, just this last year or so, there was a big party of Russian generals coming round the country, and they got taken to the zoo, maybe buying a panda because the Chinese wouldn't sell them on, something like that. My cousin says they might have been looking in the cages for a president, but she was always a cheeky monkey herself.

Uncle Percy wasn't still a keeper. Now he was head of the zoo, which he said was harder because he had to deal with visitors, who were wilder than the animals. So he met all these generals and gave them their dinner, and wine and stuff and they got merry like on holiday.

Then three or four of them had been talking, and then they spoke.

"We think we have met you," they said. "In your little house in the woods, long ago."

So my uncle looks down and sees snow on their boots still, so he knows who they are too, and that one of them was once a corporal with stripes on his arm.

"We are coming to your house again and having a big party, bringing our own bottles of brandy, you were so kind then," said the chief one. "That is what we have discussed." He had stripes still, but gold bands as well, and studs like jewels on his shoulders and a set of stars on his cap.

Well, my uncle has to do this deal with the panda, or whatever it was, so he has to agree. He doesn't care for it at all, but he can't say no.

"There's just one thing," he says. "Mind out for the cat."

"Ah yes," said the corporal-general, "some of us have not forgotten the cat."

"And now," said my uncle, "it has seven kits, just nicely grown up. But you are welcome to come."

That puts a different look on things for the Russians, so they quickly think they maybe haven't time, and one of them rubs his ear which had a dreadful scar on it still, and another rubbed his backside where some teeth met once, and off they go back to Russia.

But since it all came right about the panda, or the president, or whatever, they sent along one big collar and seven little ones, all with diamonds on, addressed to the cat and her kits.

Pussy-cat, Pussy-cat

"Pussy-cat, pussy-cat, where have you been?"
"I've been to London to visit the Queen."
  "Pussy-cat, pussy-cat, what did you there?"
"I frightened a little mouse under the chair."

❦ Mermaid ❦

To London Town, up from the sea, when a hundred years have gone by, the Mermaid comes. No one is watching for her. They have all forgotten.

She comes to the middle of the Thames at the top of the tide, the dirty tide of today.

The Mermaid too, after a hundred years, is neither beautiful nor young.

She has come up the water from the ocean-country far below. The journey is hard, the tides strong. She is old and weary. She breathes the clotted air. She coughs on city smoke.

The gentle grassy river banks are no longer there; only the concrete piers, the timber ships and iron jetties, only the flotsam and jetsam and oily slick of the world of men above the water.

"Help me," she calls, the last of all her race. "I must go up this river to my own stream or I die."

Men do not hear. Gulls look slyly at her, and they peck.

A boat-hook pushes at her.

"The tide has brought it in," say sailors, "the tide can take it out." To them she is rubbish floating on the tideway.

Along a slimy jetty, fishermen lift their hooks to let the Mermaid by, and throw cobbles to send her off. "Ugly things at sea," they say, "and never any fish these days."

Beside London Bridge the mermaid rests.

"Fend it off," says the Bridgemaster. "It's bound to smell, is that," he tells his son.

"Help me," cries the Mermaid.

Only a Boy can hear the voice; only a Boy can tell what is not weed but hair; only a Boy can see both hands and face.

The Boy is the Bridgemaster's son. He has longed for the sea all his life, and watched it from the bridge as it comes up the river each day on the tide.

He watches what comes floating by today.

"It is like an ugly thing," he says. "But it is in need."

He does not know a Mermaid would come. No one has told him. Only his father said once, "There is the blood of the sea in our veins."

The Boy had understood, and he knows there is more in his heart than the cold black river.

In his boat the Boy rows across the poisoned river towards the Mermaid.

She is by the stony bank searching for a way through.

"Help me," she says. "I must go up the little river here every hundred years, or I die, the last of all of us."

"There is no other river but this great black one," says the Boy.

"Then I die," the Mermaid says. "I come from the ocean-country far below to breathe the air, to bathe in fresh water. There are land-people among my folk, and it must be done."

"Further up there is a place where water drains away," the Boy recalls. "I do not know what river once ran there, or where it rose."

"It rises in a little lake or mere higher up among the fields," the Mermaid says. "I must go there."

"Yes," says the Boy. "I know now." He has been there. He knows a pond or lake in a green place.

A steamer hoots at him and his boat. "Take that sea-tangle out of the tideway," the shipmaster shouts. "Landlubber."

The Boy leads the Mermaid to the place he remembers, a rusty grating in the wall, where water runs with soap and slime and forgotten cast-off things. It smells, even before it joins the black Thames.

"It is not salt, and it is foul," the Mermaid says. "What has happened in a hundred years? Where are the reeds and trees, the clean banks of sand, the birds that walked in water?"

The Boy takes hammers and he breaks the bars. A tunnel lies the other side, with misty light full far away.

"Perhaps the birds sing yonder," says the Mermaid. She goes in. The Boy helps her. She weeps with fear. London rats watch and wait. Dreadful things flow down household drains.

The Boy cannot follow her. He ties up his boat and runs through the city, and beyond the wall.

In a ditch the farther side he waits. He hears the Mermaid sob as she climbs through the tunnel.

She is one hundred years today from being young. He pities her.

She crawls in sad waters. He waits.

At last she lies in the sticky ditch that the river has become. The Boy helps her along.

As they go the water deepens, and the Mermaid bobs her head below the surface.

"There is still something living in the river-country," she says. "Man has not spoilt it all."

She moves herself more easily now. She swims. The Boy no longer waits for her, but runs along the bank beside.

Age drops from the Mermaid. In the clear water she swims more slender. In a quicker current she hurries along. She raises her head, looks towards the Boy, and sings.

"Up the river, to the lake," she sings. "Then I shall be young again."

At the lake at last, the mere where the great pike bask and herons stand, the Mermaid slips back along her hundred years.

Scale by scale her past time sinks for ever; strand by strand her golden hair is cleaned and combed.

Around her come the creatures of the sweet water, smoothing and stroking her, bringing back her young beauty, her shining body, her green bright tail.

She sings. She laughs. She is joyful. The hundred years are no more on her.

The Boy comes to the margin of the mere.

He sees her on an island, lying in the sun. He has seen nothing he wants so much.

He tells her so. He says he will go with her where she goes.

"If you follow me," she says, "it will be the ocean-country for ever. Never will you come back to London and its river.

But you will be master of the seas and waves, the winds and tides."

The Boy swims to her. He picks her up. He walks with her in his arms through the city to the river, and along London Bridge.

Folk gaze at her, so young, so fair, so smooth a tail; and at him so happy and so strong.

The Bridgemaster says, "You may not jump from here. You know the rule."

But they laugh, they jump, they wave goodbye, and swim the tide to the ocean-country, the world far below.

"There is sea-blood in his veins," the Bridgemaster says. "Once in a hundred years one of us goes back."

Now that the Thames runs sweeter, his grandchildren play beneath the bridge on summer nights, sea-boys with legs, sea-girls with tails.

The Bridgemaster is not the last of all his race, the Mermaid not the last of hers.

∞ *Waterproofing* ∞

Back of the old streets in town it's all courts and little cloisters and that, and many an old mixed deal carried on, buying and selling and lading and trading, you scarcely want to be knowing.

My great-grandad, it would be, Seager was his name, looked after the graveyard of one of the churches. It isn't there now, the church, and the graveyard got built over, time out of mind. But I fancy I saw it once, little stones, and a goat in the grass and somebody with a beard, just one of those queer little yards, all gone long ago.

Well, I couldn't ever have been there, but he was, and his daughter, she looked after the goat because boys would come in and milk her dry, and by night she put her in the porch of the church, because all the services were over, and I don't know, the roof tumbling in.

My great-grandad was the sexton, but there wasn't a bell to pull or a priest to lead the amens. It was all over and done with that church by then. It was Saint Something, no I don't know any more. Maybe I never did.

I can see how it was, but I was never rightly there. It's just so long since that it comes through to me like a real thing.

This girl was my great-aunty Lizzie, and I think I saw her

once, like an old lady. But I never saw her babby brothers because they were sailors after, like their dad had been before, and she didn't like to talk about them in case she brought about how they drowned away at sea.

She was just little, she said, and saying what came into her mind when it had to be said, not knowing better. You don't at six or so.

And when she had said it she still didn't know. It only came to her long years after, when the boys had gone on their last voyage and weren't to come back. But you don't know it's their last until long after, when she put things together in her own mind.

One of the days in the churchyard, she hadn't any playmates, and she got rambling about the old church and in at the door under the cobwebs. Whether it was in the church or out in a building she cannot recall, all so ruinated about there.

There were folk in there before her, she said, like having a christening, and two babbies there in the right place, and folk gathered round.

She was cross, first, because she knew her little brothers when she saw them, and thought they were getting some treat without her sharing, so happy they were.

They were dabbling in the water, and the folk round were tipping it on them, and steam was coming up, and she thought what a Christmas washing it was.

Then she wasn't sure who all the folk were, as if they mightn't be cobwebs themselves, or this was a dream going in before her eyes. But she knew the babbies right enough.

"Now," she said, wanting to get sense, because if folk will steal milk other folk will make off with the babby that drinks it. "Now, what are you doing with my babbies?"

And the babbies splashing water out of the place where they were.

"Why," says one of the folk, "we's seething 'em."

Seething is boiling, and Lizzie knew that wasn't healthy for babbies. But if grown folk were doing it it's hard to speak against them. But she did.

"They aren't house sheets,' she said, brave as she could. "Not laundry. Babbies will scald and burn."

"Seething 'em to make 'em waterproof," says the top one of the folk doing it.

Then it came to her that she knew of something of the sort, and that fairies did it to boys so they were safe on ships if they went to sea, or dry in the water if they were ferrymen on the Thames.

So it wasn't out of the way after all, but no one had ever set eyes on it before. And they never have since, so maybe it doesn't happen any more.

And maybe if Lizzie hadn't spoken out her next words it would be happening now. I don't know. I don't think she ever told me herself.

'Well,' she said, "and what's that you're seething them in?"

"This big stone bowl does it grandly," said the top

fairy there, the one with the best-made face, daring to look plainly back. "Nearly done, they are."

"But," says Lizzie, because she knows what's what in the churchyard and the church, "you're cooking them in the font!"

That's why she thought it was a christening.

But fairies aren't christen things, and to hear of things like that is like being burnt with flames.

"Font?" says the head one. And she drops a scoop of water and claps her burnt fingers to her mouth, and all the others start screeling and bawling and away round in circles they go, knowing what they had done and what they had touched.

Lord knows, if he cares, what become of them after they whirtled out through a fallen window. But Lizzie took the little ones out of the font and carried them home, and they seemed no worse for losing their swaddle-clothes on a summer day.

But they never got quite seethed through, and Lizzie knew that all her days, but it came mostly to her for certain when they never came back, nor any of their ship, from a China voyage.

Like sailors, they were maybe drownded. And the old font, no, I don't know, I'd as likely know about the goat, so be off with you, and let the fairies be. What they don't know they ought not to hear, so remember.

∞ *The Tulip Bed* ∞

A Dutchman called Deventer, and his family came to live at the edge of Blackheath. The Mynheer was serving the King here on some business with ships and from there he could get down to the river.

He had a house belonging to the King, but it wanted more garden, which Dutchmen like, so he took in a square of heath, which the King granted him. It was meant to be for his lifetime only, because the commoners of the heath had a right to it.

He had a high brick wall built round it, because Dutch gardens are very private and folk looking in over fences spoil it for them. He had a door through on to Blackheath, if he wanted to walk there.

Then he dug the plot over with his own spade. He said there were no gardeners skilled enough in London. He laid it out in squares and rounds and put in his plants, and the folk near by knew he was growing onions in some fancy way not in neat rows. But that's the way with foreign gentlemen.

Then he was complaining to the King about his neighbours banging at his garden gate day and night, and when he got to it no one was there. The King said he must catch them at it. But the Dutchman never saw any person.

But the parson there knew who was at the door, even if knowing it wasn't church law. He said it was the pixies and that Mynheer Deventer had enclosed one of their grounds and kept them out of it. He collected old tales, he said.

Mynheer Deventer said *Yah* very many times, because he was in a foreign country and things were different. He called the bricklayers back, and a carpenter, and they built a very little door beside his own Dutchman-sized one, and he locked it and hung the keys beside it, thinking the pixies would understand.

They did, and next morning the keys had gone. But the banging stopped, and the garden was peaceful.

His garden grew. How high a wall doesn't matter, because folk will stand on each other's' shoulders to spy over the top. So it was known how the garden grew very pretty in a year or two with the new flower called Turks-head, or tulip, very fresh to the country that year. The garden was full of them, yellow and red and brown, filling all the squares and rounds and garden-bed shapes, among the little bushes of box and other sweet shrubs.

This is what Mynheer Deventer told the King. By the little door there was a gate-keeper pixy, which no man could see, but it kept away cats and dogs and weasels and stoats and any harmful thing, only letting in and out the young pixy mothers with their babes.

Also, the Mynheer said, these were the only tulips in the world to have a sweet scent all night long.

It is not known what the King thought.

The parson, and one or two local gentlemen and their

ladies were let into the house to see the garden closer. They smelled the flowers, and late in the evening they also heard some sort of sound.

The King's master of song came, and heard music. He wrote down a few lines of tune, and they could be heard whistled in the city for a year or two.

He would have written some of it for church, but the bishops would not let him use pixy melody.

These grand people heard a little and smelled somewhat, but only the Mynheer's children saw what else there was.

They wrote it down later, but the parson said they had made it up from what he had said about old tales. But the children said that the old tales were proved.

The garden was a nursery, they said, and the flowers made music to rest the babes while the mothers slept and rested, combed their hair, and mended their wings. Then they kissed their babies, and in the morning early they would troop out of the garden back to their homes hidden on the heath.

Mynheer and Mynfrow believed them, but the parson wrote to the King that these people were not acting like Christians. The King remembered what he had been told by the Mynheer about the gate-keeper pixy, and said the Mynheer and his family must go, and back to Holland they went. That was before that war, but did not cause it.

Then, instead of taking the wall down and giving back that enclosed piece of Blackheath, which he had promised the commoners he would do, the King let a park-keeper live in the house and grow herbs for the King's table. So the tulips went, and there was parsley instead, and onions, as was first supposed, in long rows.

And he broke down the little door so that his dogs could come in and out. All these things made the garden no longer a nursery, and perhaps a pixy had been hurt or a baby killed in the new work, or the ground was now dangerous. But from that time on the parsley drooped and withered, the onions rotted as they grew, and at the last there was only the black soil and no living thing.

In time the pixies left the whole of the heath, and they were the last pixies in the whole of London. This was a few hundred years ago.

It is said that the graves of a certain family in Holland are tended by unseen hands, and that on them grow small tulips, of an old kind that have a scent. No other tulips have that. But if they are picked the scent goes at once. Perhaps that is where the pixies went, and the graves are those of Mynheer Deventer and his family who had been kind to them.

As for the garden at Blackheath, the house has long gone, and the brick wall is a shadow on the turf, and inside no strange flowers grow. Only now and then on a dewy morning the pattern of the old garden shows on the ground until the sun dries it away.

∽ *The Two Giants* ∽

L
ong ago there were giants in the land, not many but some, left over from the first ages of the world. There came a time when they were all thought to be dead, which was a pity because they made reasonable servants. Indeed some people treated them as slaves.

They were strong and willing workers, and if they were fed and kept warm they did not complain. In fact they could not complain, because they could not speak. They understood what was said to them, if it was not too difficult, but their big mouths and strong throats could not make words.

Among ordinary men many parents wished their own children did not learn to speak. But that's the same now as it was then.

There were no more giants because they stopped having baby giants. There were no more of them being mothers or fathers. That tribe was dying out. It was taking hundreds of years because they live lengths of time like that.

But the tribes of men went on increasing, and that led to problems about having enough land to live on and getting enough to eat from it. There were fights. There were quarrels. There were wars, when twenty warriors each side would stand up and shout at each other and then throw stones. They might even come and hit the other side with sticks. They had good big words meaning 'enemy'.

"I wish we had a giant or two to frighten them," said Uthred's father. "That would be some good."

Because the men from the north were getting near and had taken some wild pigs he had had his eye on.

"Giants, ugh," said little Dariel. She was a fierce little girl. "I would bang the giant if he looked at me."

"Hm," said her father. "Don't do that if you meet one. They are very big."

"But there aren't any," said Uthred. "And if there was, he can have you."

"There is a much worse problem with the men from the north," said their mother. "Stay close to home. We hear they eat children, and what's more they cook them too."

So it wasn't always safe to go roaming about. But young Uthred, not taking much notice of that, went with his little sister Dariel right away from their hut and into the trees, and began to play their own games.

"Giants," said Uthred. "No such thing."

"Bang, he's dead," said Dariel, hitting the ground with a stick to show what she would do.

They were working at the same time, finding things to eat and putting them in a bark basket to take home, mushrooms, and nuts, and that nice moss, and some little roots. They ate the large fat beetles as soon as they found them, though, because otherwise the beetles climbed out of the basket and ran away.

So the pair of them went a bit further off than they should have gone. And then Dariel stood up and waved to some people, and the people waved back.

But the people were not mothers and fathers. They were bad-tempered tribesmen from the north. Too late Dariel remembered that she would be eaten.

So she ran away. She hoped she was running home, but she had no idea where that was.

And the people from the north probably thought she looked quite tender, and that if they cooked Uthred for a bit he would be tender too.

Uthred followed Dariel. He had been told to look after her.

They went up a hill, because that was the only way left. "We don't live up here," said Uthred.

"We've moved," said Dariel, because her mind worked very quickly. "And there's a house."

It wasn't their house. It wasn't a house at all. It was a cave in the chalk. But it had a fire outside it, like a house, and something was cooking on a stick. And there were big chairs to sit on, so there must be big people there.

They came out of the cave. The big people were giants. They were not full-sized giants but children giants. And their dinner was burning.

They did not know what to do about that. They were thinking of putting the fire out, because their minds worked rather slowly. But Uthred knew it would be more sensible to move the dinner away.

However, enemy tribesmen from the north were just behind him, so there was not much he could do but keep on running.

"Just run in a friendly way," he told Dariel. But she was puffed out and all she could do was go to the grownest-up person there was and hold on to his knee.

The young giant probably thought she was a doll. He liked her. He patted her on the head with a huge hand. She was very sensible, and shrieked and pointed at the men from the north.

The young giant put her on a chair, picked up a tree, or a spear, or something, and went out to meet the men from the north.

The men from the north ran away, shouted a few rude things, and went home. Well, home was really far in the north, so they went to their latest camp.

That piece of war did not take long. So Uthred was able to rescue the giants' dinner by taking the great big kebab-style skewer from the fire and putting out the flames. The giants were having scorched pork.

They were happy to share it. Dariel had not seen a giant before, but she knew she did not need to be afraid of them. It's really giants who were afraid of men. She and Uthred shared their dinner and the giants didn't say a word.

Then things got rather horrid, because the men from the north came back and started a giant hunt by throwing stones and shouting and chanting in a vulgar way. They had bagpipes too, which sounded very cruel.

The two giants began to cry. They were young, and they were lost, and they were the last of all their race. Uthred thought their parents had already been killed by people, but it was not easy to tell.

"We shall take them home," he said. "They will fight for us."

"They are too frightened," said Dariel, stroking the arms of one of them, She did this by standing on the chair and smiling and reaching up.

"They can be trained," said Uthred. He thought he knew all that stuff. "Like dogs. They will roar."

But for the time being they all ran away and hid the other side of the hill. The northern tribesmen went home too, because it was now raining and not a day for fighting.

Next it was a night for Uthred and Dariel not being warm or dry, down by the big river.

But in the morning Uthred saw smoke, and led all four of them to their own village. Only his mother was at home, and she had not been happy. She thought they had been caught and eaten. The men and the other women had gone to eat some children from the north, just to make things fair.

"We are very well," said Uthred. "And we have brought some friends to play."

He was also jealous about his father eating other children. After all, he could eat Dariel if he wanted to be useful.

"Giants," said their mother. "There are no giants left. What are their names?" She was not frightened of the giants either. Giants might accidentally sit on you, but they were not greedy or vicious.

"What is your name?" Dariel asked her giant. She was riding on his shoulders.

"Gug," said her giant, not able to talk.

"Mugug," said Uthred's. They did their best, but no one knew what they had meant to say.

"We had better start training them," said his mother. "Gug, go and fetch water from the river. I am making acorn porridge."

And Mugug was sent to gather firewood.

"Your father will train them to be soldiers," Uthred's mother said.

Before the end of the day his father came back with the rest of the people. They had not had a very good fight because the northern men had hidden and thrown rocks from out of sight, which is hardly a proper way to fight. "Real men come out into the open," said Uthred's father.

"Or," he said, "they send a giant out to do it for them. That's technology."

They had eaten nothing all day, not a nut, not a child.

They were glad to see giants again, shambling about all hairy, and not much more smelly than their own friends and relations.

"Gug belongs to me," said Dariel. "Mugug belongs to Uthred. Don't frighten them."

"Someone has to fight," said her father. "That's work experience."

"Not with my toys," said Dariel. And that was that.

Nothing came out the way it was planned. The giants never had to fight. But they thought of building a great big ditch to keep the northern tribes away. They built it by the river, and when they took out the last lumps of rock the water came right round the village and they got their feet wet and cried.

They would keep watch all night, as well. And when the

enemy threw stones then Gug would throw them back very hard. But if the enemy threw lumps of wood Mugug would keep them. In this way the enemy learned only ever to throw useful firewood, because it did not hurt on the way back.

The giants grew bigger, and bigger, until they were twice as tall as men. Then nobody threw anything at them.

The enemy began to forget to throw anything at all, quite half the time. In fact, once or twice he actually waved in a friendly way as he went by, and seemed to have given up eating children. No one could be sure, because there weren't any children anyway.

Uthred grew as tall as he could.

Dariel grew up too, and when she did so the enemy kept coming to look at her, as she sat and combed her hair with some twigs. At last one of the northern boys came along with a bark basket of acorns and honey and goat-milk, and stared and stared across the ditch.

"It's love," said Dariel, blushing a lot. "I quite like honey, so perhaps I'd better say yes. I'll pack my things and my giant."

"It can't be you he's after," said Uthred. "Look at you. You're a girl, or something. It'll be Gug he wants."

Of course Gug would have to go with Dariel. But just as much Gug had to stay with Mugug. But matters were solved by all the men getting together and sorting out which bits of land the two tribes would own.

"I'm sorry to cause all this trouble," said Dariel. "But he won't go away unless I go with him."

"It's all very interesting," said her father. "We've begun to think it might be nicer to go visiting and have drinks at the

weekend, than throw stones at each other all week. And
they have quite super dinners, a lovely thing with marinated
slugs, for instance. Anyway, we've worked things out." And
he began to explain where everybody could hunt or grow
tasty nettles or that crunchy grass with nubbly seeds.

And then Uthred began to think that a girl over there
might be nice to hang around with, but of course he could
neither take Mugug with him, or leave him behind.

Then a tribe from the west began to throw stones and
small pointed bits of wood called arrows, which stuck into
you. Also, they were short and dark and sang in an eerie
way, and didn't know how to carry on at all and might be
dangerous as well as foreign.

So Uthred's tribe and their first enemies all came to live
behind the ditch, and Gug and Mugug built a fort in the
middle.

And so it went on, until the new enemy became friendly.
Now the new enemy tends to drive taxis round London
fiercely. Uthred's descendents ride about in the taxis, and
Dariel's lot tends to make the rules.

Gug and Mugug lasted many years. Now they stand
outside a building, ready to defend it if necessary. But all
they have ever said is their own names. And this story must
be true, because you can see them any time, and hear them
say their names at midnight.

But don't throw stones.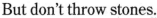

‿ ℐhe Tale of the Blue Pig ‿

The Mayor of Whitechapel sent a message to the Chairman of Stepney Council, saying, "Send me a blue pig with a black tail, or else . . ."
You know how it is with messages these days.
The Chairman replied, " Thank you for your letter of the 14th ult. I have not got one; and if I had . . ."
When the Mayor got this answer he flew into a great rage, and declared war against Whitechapel. You know how it is these days, digging up the roads, refusing planning, offering bribes, and all that political stuff. For years fighting went on, and the people of Whitechapel did not dare go over into Stepney, and the people of Stepney went shopping in Poplar, which did not happen to be at war.
In the end the Lord Chief Justice and two molecatchers who hadn't been paid, took them both to court.
"It was like this," said the Mayor. "I sent a friendly letter . . ."
"The relevant document," said the Chairman."
"We never got paid for our moles," said the molecatchers.
"Shut up, all of you," said the Lord Chief Justice. "I want to get home to my tea."
"He told me to send him a blue pig with a black tail, or else . . ." said the Chairman.

"I understand that," said the Lord Chief Justice. "Very threatening, and a war is only self-defence after all. Explain it, Mayor of Whitechapel."

"Why," said the Mayor, "I meant a blue pig with a black tail, or else some other colour. But what did he mean by his warlike message: 'I have not got one, and if I had . . .'?"

"My meaning was simple enough," said the Chairman of Stepney. "If I had had such a pig I would have sent it. Wasn't it for a barbecue at Tower Bridge?"

"It seems to me," said the Lord Chief Justice, "that you need better ribbons in your typewriters. Now you can both buy the other a drink, and you can each buy me one."

The molecatchers got quite tipsy and went home and barbecued their latest catches.

All in the Dumps

We are all in the dumps
For diamonds are trumps;
    The kittens are gone to St Paul's!
The babies are bit,
    The moon's in a fit,
And the houses are built without walls.

∞ℳr Jamrach's Tiger ∞

In October, 1857, Mr Jamrach purchased a lot of animals from a ship arriving from abroad, and among them a large tiger in a den. During the voyage the weather had been very stormy, and the sea had frequently washed over the decks, the tiger's den partaking in the general wetting.

When the ship arrived at the London Docks, the den was put in a van and placed in Mr Jamrach's yard, with the bars towards the wall. The den having been thus placed, Mr Jamrach walked away, when on turning round a few minutes afterwards, he saw that the tiger had reared herself up on her hind legs, and a board giving way to her pressure, he perceived with horror that she was coming loose out of the den.

In a few moments the board, which was quite rotten, "let go", and out walked the tiger through the yard gate into the street. A little boy, about nine years old, happened to be playing in the street. This little boy, thinking that the tiger was a big dog, walked up to her, and began patting her; the tiger then turned her head and seized the boy by the shoulder with her tremendous fangs. Jamrach, immediately running up, grasped the tiger by the loose skin of her neck, but, although a very strong and powerfully-built man, he could not hold the beast, who immediately started off down the street at a gallop, carrying the boy in her mouth as a cat would a mouse, Jamrach holding on tight all the time to the tiger's neck, and keeping up with long strides by her side, like a groom by the side of a runaway horse.

Finding that his hold was giving way, he managed to slip the tiger's hind leg from under her, and she fell to the ground. Jamrach instantly threw his whole weight down on her, and letting go the skin of her neck, fastened his two thumbs behind her ears with a firm grip.

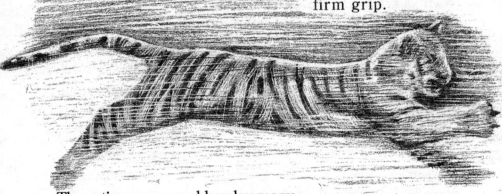

There tiger, man, and boy lay many minutes altogether in a heap, the man gripping the tiger, the tiger (still holding the boy in his fangs) all the while suffering great pain from the pressure of Jamrach's hands, and from impeded respiration. After a time one of Jamrach's men was actually bold enough to put his head round the corner to see if he could render his master assistance. Jamrach cried out, "Bring me a crow-bar!"

The man got a crowbar and struck the tiger three severe blows on the nose with it, which made her drop the child from her mouth. Jamrach then sent him for some ropes; these ropes, of course, in the confusion became entangled, and the tiger, watching her opportunity, sprang up, and getting loose, ran back again up the street, Jamrach after her, crowbar in hand: she bolted immediately round the corner, through the yard gate, and leaped into her den, from which she had escaped. Once inside she cowered down and lay as quiet as possible.

The child was, strange to say, not much hurt. He had only a bite on the shoulder, which got well in eight days. The poor little fellow, however, was so terribly frightened that he never spoke for four hours.

Mr Jamrach got the worst of this affair; for having had to fight the tiger, he then had to fight the lawyers, and the whole business cost him, in damages and law expenses, over 300*l*. He had caught, in fact, a Tartar; for, said he, "There was a lawyer as well as a tiger inside the tiger's skin," and he had first to tackle the tiger, and then lawyer afterwards – too much for any man's nerves.

This story of the child and tiger got into all the newspapers, and Mr Edmonds, seeing the account, came up from Birmingham (where his menagerie was then being exhibited) and bought the tiger for 200*l*. He put it in his collection, and advertised it as: "The tiger that swallowed the child in Ratcliff Highway."

Everybody went to see it, of course, and his purchase turned out a good speculation for about four days, but no longer; for this very tiger, when the men were gone to dinner, put her claw into the partition of her den, pushed out the partition, and walked into the neighbouring den, in which dwelt a lion worth a large sum of money. The tiger immediately attacked the lion, catching him by the throat, and in a few minutes killed him. This same tiger is, I believe, still being exhibited in Edmonds's menagerie.

I really think, and doubtless my readers will agree with me, that Mr Jamrach deserves very great credit for attacking his fierce and runaway tiger single-handed, and rescuing the poor little boy. I record the story as a testimony to his courage and pluck.

In my grandmother's childhood this story was folklore, to the extent that she would add a false verisimilitude to it, saying she "once knew the boy who was caught, and if your grandfather had not come along, who knows?"

The story was recounted in these words by Frank Buckland, at the time, and printed by him in a book of Natural History.

❧ *Jack of Heathrow* ❧

Once upon a time a boy called Jack lived with his mother at Heathrow, in the desolation of that lonely and distant place where only the wind blew and the hares ran.

They were very poor, and the mother got her living by spinning. First she had to gather the wool where it hung in bush and bramble. Then she had to wash it in the River Colne. Next she would comb and card it, and then set her wheel going.

So when she had wool it was work day and night, and when she had none there was no food for her and Jack.

Jack was too idle to think. All summer long he would lie in the sun, and all winter keep close to the fire, while his mother went out in all weathers. Jack did nothing to help, only complained if his belly was not filled two and three times a day.

This was all very well when he was little. But there came a time when he was old enough to see to some things for himself.

"You are big enough and ugly enough to find some work," his mother told him one day when he had eaten both potatoes that were dinner for the whole household. "Here you are in the world, and making nothing of it. Off you go

in the morning and do not come again without something
you have earned. I am too old to manage for us both, so you
must get in the way of managing for yourself."

The next day, or perhaps the one after when he found his
mother truly meant what she said, Jack went seeking work,
and got sixpennorth of it at a farm the topside of Heathrow.

It would do him for a week, he thought, and ran away
home with it. But when he got home the coin was nowhere
to be found.

"Well you are no good still," said his mother. "How did
you come to lose it?"

"It was crossing the River Crane," said Jack. "My hand
was too cold to hold the sixpenny bit, and down in the water
it went."

"Next time," said his mother, "put it in your pocket. That
is big enough and empty enough."

"I will," said Jack, "I will."

"Will you now?" said his mother.

The next work Jack got was with a cowkeeper, away over
towards Stanwell, another fine swinging walk and all in the
rain too.

This time his wage was not money but a jar of milk.

Jack thought of his mother once, and did not drink it
straight off; and he thought of her twice and put the jar in
his pocket.

So when he got home he went to take the jar out, and
somehow on the way it had tipped over, and somehow in the
wet he had not felt the milk run away to the ground.

"Well," said his mother, "it was a kind thought, as far as it
went. If we had a cat, which I should well like, that would
lick it up from there, but we can't. Next time carry it on

your head."

"I will, Mother," said Jack. "Indeed I will."

"Will you now?" said his mother.

Next he worked at the dairy in Bedfont, and for his wage he was given a cream cheese in its muslin and a cabbage leaf.

He took notice of what his mother said now. He walked home with the cream cheese on his head. It was not comfortable, "But it is what she said," he remembered.

The cheese had run into his hair and matted it. It had run down his neck. It had spilt on his shoulders. The muslin was empty; the cabbage leaf was hollow.

"But you must use your sense," said his mother. "I downright despair of you every day, Jack."

"And is there nothing to eat?" asked Jack.

"Nothing," said his mother. "Next time carry it in your hands, gently."

"I will, Mother," said Jack. "I shall not forget."

"Won't you, Jack, won't you?" said his mother.

Jack was next at the bakery by Hatton Cross, and since he got his dinner there of a new pie, the baker gave him a fine tom-cat, which Jack knew his mother would like, to drink spilt milk.

He did what he was told. He carried Puss carefully in his hands. The cat had not heard what Jack's mother said. He did not care to be carried. He scraped with his forepaws, he scratched with his back, he struck with his tail and he bit with his teeth, and he shouted dreadfully. Until he fell from Jack's bleeding arms and went off to catch a hare if he could.

"Ah well," said his mother, bandaging his arms, "next

time tie it with a piece of cord and bring it along like that. At least you will not be scratched."

"I will, Mother, I will," said Jack.

"I expect you will," said his mother.

The next day the butcher at Sipson Green took him on. Since Jack was getting used to working he did well at the shop, and his wages consisted of a large shoulder of mutton.

"And I just need a piece of cord," said Jack. "My mother says."

That was soon done, and Jack on his way home with the mutton on a lead like a dog, walking through the dust and weeds and mud, across stones and ruts, and being hunted by dogs.

"Mother knows best," said Jack.

His mother was not pleased at the rag of dirty bone he took to her.

"You are a dolt," she said.

"I did what you told me, Mother," said Jack.

"Yes, indeed," said his mother. "But next time carry it on your shoulder and bring it home clean."

"I shall do that," said Jack. "My shoulder, yes."

"I wonder," said his mother.

The next day he worked in the mill at Harmondsworth, but instead of a bag of flour the miller gave him an old donkey to take home for company.

Jack had a hard time with it. He was a strong lad, but the donkey had never been carried on a boy's shoulder before, which is how Jack took him across Heathrow.

He was halfway home when he met the King of Staines on his way to visit the King of Hounslow. He had his daughter Polly with him, a poor girl who could not speak or hear and had never laughed, though they had tried tickling her. So she was the sorry thing in the king's life, and he never made her happy, and no one would have her as a wife, because quiet is one thing, but miserable another. But Polly was pretty when she was not ugly with sulking.

"Well, Jack," said the king, with his arm round the poor girl, who would not look up. "How is it?"

"Thirsty work," said Jack, trying to get the donkey's legs under his arm. "This is a tricky trade."

He was trying to gather all the limbs of the donkey under control and not be bitten by the beast.

"I have to get it right," said Jack. "Mother says." But he was not managing very well, and the donkey laughed his great braying hee-haw.

Polly looked up at the sound and saw what Jack was doing. It was the first funny thing she had ever seen, and she gave her first laugh, and her second, and her third, and a whole life of them until tears ran down her cheeks, and still she laughed.

And then she was able to speak like any other girl. So the day ended with the donkey under the girl, Jack's mother leading it, the king holding its tail, and Jack leading the way to Feltham church. There he married the girl, and she's still talking.

His mother said, "It's how you bring them up that matters. He's a good and obedient boy."

"I will be," said Jack.

"I don't doubt it," said his mother.

And from that day to this Jack farms half the kingdom of the King of Staines, his mother lives in a tower, the donkey is retired, and still nothing grows on Heathrow.

∞ Mawkinhead ∞

Simple people live out east of London, and the man who tried to fence the Goodwin Sands and put a farm there was one of them. It's the best way to be. The government didn't like that, and sent out a boat and all the coppers were sick as hell over the side but they said all the same, "Come along with us."

He didn't come that easy, and he wasn't seasick, standing on his own farm. "Get out of my twelve-acre," he told them, "that's my spring wheat you got your anchor in."

But they took him to police court at Dover, where they wouldn't listen but sent him to magistrates at Maidstone.

"I got my subsidies from the EEC," he told the magistrates, "and my quotas and my permits. It's Europe, is it not?"

"Get on with you," they said and locked him in a cell, "grow your spring wheat in there." Because they were farmers too.

"It's better land for maslin," he said, "barley and peas." But they locked the door. "It's a dry season," he said, because it never rained.

Next they had him to London, and he looked at the Thames and he said, "You could stock that with Downland sheep," but they didn't, even when he explained about stock payments.

They had him into a great courtroom and he looked round and said, "You could get a grand lot of intervention butter in here."

But they said, "You are trying to bribe us."

They put him in the dock. "This is a poor sort of loose box," he said. "Regulations call for straw and hay and water and a groom."

So they gave him two grooms. One was a copper, and the other a jailkeeper, and they put a chain on him. "Well now, you'll have to lead me about," he said.

Then everyone stood up. "It's going to rain at last," said our man. "It's a sure sign when the cows stand up."

But it wasn't that. It was the judge coming in, all dressed in his robes and so on.

"Who's she?" asked the man, when he saw his honour's stockings and buckles and a long sort of frock. "She's none too pretty for a wife, but if she brings me some land I'll have her."

"Silence," said the clerk. "What do you plead?"

The man thought it was an auction sale. "Subject to veterinary inspection," he said, "I'll go to fifty shillings."

"Guilty," said the clerk, a deaf old dog.

So then a lawyer got up and started asking about the farm on Goodwin Sands, how many acres and how many gates and field numbers and plans and registration and leys of permanent grass.

That's all simple for a farmer, and never bothered our man in the dock. But he didn't think it was any business of the lawyer, and just wanted to be down at Goodwin farming and making hay and shooting rabbits in the tide.

"I know all that, Mawkinhead," he said, seeing the tufty

little curls of horsehair lawyers wear to cover their baldness.

The judge rapped on the desk. "We won't have none of that," he said, "that's not polite or ought to be said. Contempt of court, that is."

"And you change your barber and all, miss," said the man. "I don't like your hair-do neither, and I might just withdraw from the bidding and let you find someone else."

They thought that was shocking. They locked him away right at the bottom of the jail, and there was plenty of straw to lie on, and not much else, and it was years and years before they remembered him, and that was because the subsidies and set-asides and Sites-of-Special-Scientific-Interest money began to pile up in the bank and getting in the way, and a grand crop.

But when he got in the same dock he still wanted for straw and hay.

"Where's Mawkinhead?" he asked, but they didn't know what he meant. It was modern times now, and all the judges looked like men, and even the lawyers, and there wasn't a wig in sight.

"That Mawkinhead business is quite forgot," the judge said, "along of what you said we changed all that. But you can't farm Goodwin Sands no more, that's disallowed after next week. You get to keep all the money, though, because you farmed it until now, and that's the law of Europe."

"That's what I said all the time," said the man. "Baldy."

"Now don't spoil it," said the judge.

So the man went home, richer than he started. And since he can't farm, he runs the Goodwin Sands golf course out there in the middle of the Channel, if you want a game. Or you can shoot rabbits in the rough.

The Man, the Dwarf, the bag

Once there was a wicked dwarf, but it was in those days, not now at all. The dwarf had one trick only, and by that trick he got his living. He had a leather bag, with a laced mouth done up like a boot. He would come to a house and put the bag down outside, then he would climb into it, hunch himself down, and draw the laces tight from inside.

Soon someone would be picking up the bag and taking it into the house, any house, out of curiosity, or perhaps to steal it. But the bag could not be opened, except by the dwarf from inside. He would be in there, and hear the knives and scissors going at the outside without making a scratch on the surface. In the end the noises would stop, and the bag be left for the night in a room of the house, or in the town hall, or anywhere.

When everything was quiet the dwarf would come out, lay hold of what he fancied to steal, and take it into the bag with him. It was no ordinary bag, and he could put into it a great deal more than you would think it could hold. No one would know the thief, or who had been at the larder and finished the goose, and drunk the milk or the ale. One quiet night, when the bag had been forgotten, the dwarf would climb out again, pick it up, and leave the house. That was his livelihood, ...ling in the one town and selling in another.

At last he ...et with a man no better than himself. The dwarf ha...ome up to a castle, where he thought there might ... good pickings of gold and maybe cream with it too in ... kitchen. So he prepared himself, and laid the bag ...side the road towards the castle door. Along came the man, whose name was Grinday, and he was a thief. He picked up the bag and tried to open it there and then, but could make nothing of the job.

"Something or nothing, I'll make a chance of it," Grinday said to himself. "I'll ask at the castle if it's theirs." He went to the castle door with the bag tucked under his arm. Sweeping his hair tidy, he told his tale, giving a name that was not his, making out he was a true traveller, come miles out of his road with something he thought belonged to the lord of the place. So he was let in for the night, putting the bag against his bed and forgetting about it. It had done its work, for Grinday and for the dwarf.

The dwarf knew nothing of this. He
waited until all was quiet, came out,
and began to look for something to
make off with. But just at the same
time the man Grinday was about the
same task, creeping from place to
place. He came on the dwarf putting the castle silver in the
bag. Grinday watched, amazed to see how much went in.
For himself, he only ever took what he could carry away
next morning before its loss was noticed.

But for that night he said nothing, and did nothing. In the
morning he went on his way, taking the bag with him, and
the dwarf in it. He made his way to town, considering what
to do, how to make the best use of what he had, and to
master the dwarf. No matter how he tried he could not
break into the bag to steal the contents for himself.

A night or two later, in a thieves' shelter in the town, not
knowing where he was, the dwarf came out, bringing his
silver with him.

Now, all the time he had been breaking the silver up so
that it was little more than dust, so that he could sell it
without being found out. The dwarf counted his gains, put
them back in the bag, and sold his loot to a silversmith. But
when he came back, and had the bag open, ready to go into
it again, the man stepped forward and caught him, dwarf in
the one hand, bag in the other.

"Now," he said, "I have you. You have a fine trick here,
and you and it can enter my service, and between us we
shall do everything in the world."

The dwarf saw that he was caught out of his home, and
that there was nothing to do but give in. He said, though he

did not mean it, "I have for a long time been looking for a skilful partner whom I could trust. We shall indeed go about the world together, and I am sure we shall do very well."

"So we shall," said Grinday. But he thought to himself, only if I am master.

"But you must let me into the bag," said the dwarf, "or I shall be of no use to you. It is made from the magic relics of ancient dwarf kingdoms, and I cannot live far from it, nor can it stray far from me."

"I wish to keep you happy," said the man. "But I cannot let you hide in there. I will let you in, but first I will take the laces out, so that I can open the bag as I need to, and take you in or out. That will be our partnership."

So that was the arrangement they came to, and they went about the world together, neither of them getting the best of it, because there was little of honesty in either of them.

All the dwarf could think about was how to get away from the man and have his bag back, and all the man thought about was how to be rid of the dwarf and have the bag to himself.

They went about, and the dwarf did the work and ran the risks, the man spent the money, and never had such a time in his life, a good companion to all he met.

In the end, instead of knowing himself to be a humble thieving villain he began to think he should be grander, and took to going about in a coach in full comfort. The dwarf would be strapped on top, and without his laces the wind and rain and snow came in on him. There he lay, sorrowing for what had become of him, and scheming to get the laces back, because they were fully half the magic of the bag.

The grandness of Grinday brought a bold idea to his mind, one that he could not do without the dwarf. They came to London, where the king had his palace. Before they reached it Grinday had the coach painted fresh, with a coat of arms, and gave out that he was a prince of Hungary, come into the country looking for a bride.

"You and I," Grinday said to the dwarf, "will be able to live happily in our different ways, and your back shall always be on a cushion."

"And my laces?" asked the dwarf. "What of them?"

"They shall be hung on the wall," said the man; but the dwarf did not believe him.

The king had one child, a daughter who was not yet married. And where there is a princess there is a kingdom, better than riches. It was towards the end of those times, and princes were uncommon. It was natural that when a prince of Hungary should come to town there was great talk of the matter. Before long there came an invitation for Grinday to live at the Tower for a while.

There they went. The princess did not see him, or he the princess, but it was enough that the man was in the palace, with the dwarf and the bag.

That night, as they supped, Grinday said to the chamberlain, "Tomorrow my people are bringing from Dover a quantity of gold, which I always carry with me. Will you be good enough to tell me of a safe place where I may put it?"

"The treasury of the Tower is very secure, Your Highness," said the chamberlain. Grinday then said he would prefer to look before entrusting his wealth to a strange vault. After supper they went down to look.

The man pretended to examine the walls to see how strong they were, and he was glad to find there was a way for the dwarf to come up from the room with the bag. So he said the place would be safe enough, and just for the night might he leave this bag here? "It has some precious things in it," he said.

He had seen the king's own treasure laid out, ready for the taking, and this the way to take it.

The chamberlain laid the bag on a shelf with his own hand, and locked the vault door behind as they came out. That was the first part dealt with.

Instead of sleeping, Grinday went out of the window and waited by the castle wall. In the darkness there came the dwarf, carrying the bag full of gold from the vault, fuller than you could think, but being magic, not heavy. Grinday took the bag and rode out of town. By the river he hired a wagon, tipped out the gold into it, and arranged for it to be brought to the palace the next day.

Great amazement was caused by the wagon of gold. No one outside the Tower had seen so much together at a time, and never in one wagon. Grinday told the carter not to worry about fallen coins, because there were plenty more. The people followed the cart, picking up the angels, marks, and shillings that fell through the cracks in the floor.

It was not Grinday's money. He had no need to worry.

The king was impressed by such richness, and by a prince who did not mind losing gold coins. He thought it a foolish thing to do, but it meant the prince was rich. So he wondered pretty much what he was meant to wonder, whether his daughter might not be a suitable bride.

That was the first day. Night after night, for a week, the

man and the dwarf met in the dark, and day after day a cartload of gold came through the streets.

On the last day the prince said to the king, "You will have heard that I am perhaps looking for a royal bride."

The king said he had heard so; and that was the way the matter was started. It went on further when Grinday confessed that he had come on purpose to woo the princess, and brought so much of his wealth, though by no means all.

"I have a mind to settle in this land," he said, "and perhaps take half the kingdom when your majesty wishes to have the burden of it from your shoulders."

"I see," said the king. "Something has to be done, after all."

So it was arranged that the man should marry the princess, but no one asked her about it. That is the way it was in those days.

That night the dwarf said, "Why can you not be content with all the royal treasure we have stolen? We could be soon away to another part of the world, and perhaps you could give me back my laces and my bag and let me go."

"Not yet," said the man. "Not yet. Remember, that to a dwarf gold is all that matters, but to a man something else is important, and that is, what he has made of himself. It is better than gold to marry a princess. There is nothing more a man can want."

"That's as may be," said the dwarf, because that was all nonsense to him. "Good store of money is all a dwarf needs."

"Well, perhaps there is one doubt," said Grinday. "So far I have not set eyes on the princess. I wonder whether I would wish to marry an ugly one, with a bad temper and

biting tongue. I think it would be safest if I looked at her before going further with this affair. We can always leave and not come back. But this is what we shall do. I shall get into the bag, and you will take me to the princess and let me see her and talk with her. Then I shall know."

"That I shall do willingly," said the dwarf. "I do not wish you to be unhappy. But before I put you in the bag you will have to give me the laces, because you cannot have all the power."

"That is a small enough thing to do," said Grinday, bringing the laces from his weskit pocket and handing them over.

"I will go and find the best way," said the dwarf. But he did not go towards the princess's rooms, for of course he did not wish Grinday to be happy. Instead he went down to the woman who kept the pigs, and told her straight out that the prince wished to marry her, and that she should be

clean and wholesome and in one of the apartments of the
Tower in an hour's time.

That was arranged. In those days it might happen. The
dwarf was pleased, because the woman who kept the pigs
was extremely ugly as a human, but not out of the way for a
pig, with a temper that would boil swill, and a tongue that
would slice bacon.

The dwarf dressed himself as a tame ape, which was often
a sort of servant in those days, and carried the bag with the
man in it to the palace room. In an hour the pigwoman
came there too.

The man came out of the bag when the pigwoman was not
expecting him, so she was startled, and when he saw her so
was Grinday. They both began shouting, until the man was
afraid for his life and jumped from the window. The dwarf
got the bag back, and the pigwoman went back to her pigs.

The man fell into the River Thames and was taken down
by the tide. The dwarf saw him go, and fancied himself as
good as a prince now.

"He's out of the way," he said. "I wonder if there is
anything in what he says about marrying a princess."

He called a servant and gave an order in the prince's
name, to take the bag to the princess's rooms. He got into
it, laced it up, and was taken directly to the princess, as a
present.

Now, the way things are in palaces, every rumour gets
around. So the princess knew the prince was to visit her,
and would certainly send a present just before. So she was
ready for him.

She knew that the prince was tall and dark, though
perhaps a little older than she would have chosen; but there

were few fairy-tale princes in those days.

So she was not at all ready for a little rusty, dirty dwarf to come out of the bag and say he was the true prince, and all the wealth was his.

She did three things, all wise. She screamed once, stamped her foot once, took up the tongs from beside the fire and got the dwarf by the ear with them, and pitched him from the window, once, before he knew it.

The bag was sent down to be thrown away, but they found that it would hold all the rubbish itself, and they use it for that to this day.

The chamberlain and the treasurer counted up the king's treasure and found it all in the vaults, except for a few coins. It was in the wrong place, but it was thought the king had been counting it.

There was great fury because the prince had left with his treasure without saying farewell. The pigwoman tells no tales, the princess married a perfectly good tailor after a time. The man Grinday and the dwarf floated down the Thames together and, who knows, they may still be at sea. And the kingdom got what it deserved.

∽ *Upminster* ∾

There was a London man, there was his lady wife. They'd naught to do that day, and thought they'd take a walk, a stroll, and entertain their minds.

"Oh, Mr Binks," said she, "where shall we go?"

"It matters not," he said, "we'll see when we arrive."

But his lady wife was not content with that. Her mind on it was neither happy nor entire.

"Please take more thought," she said. "It's best to know."

So he thought, and he thought again.

"It matters not," he said. "There and back to see how far it is will do."

"But where?" she asked. "You see I have to dress the part and my perfect looks be right."

"You look ever perfect," said the London man. "I chose you just for that."

"And you loved me true," his wife remembered.

"And there was that," he said. "Shall we be off?"

"Where do we go?" she asked him once again. "Don't give me surprises now, or disappointment there will be."

"So there will," he said. "I've heard of many places round the town. Is it excitement and is it thrills? Or is it pretty landscapes while we feed the ducks? Or shall we see the zoo or visit houses smart?"

"All those I have done," she said. "Is it fish-net or many denier fine? Is it flannelette of bombazine?"

"I've made my mind," he said. "We'll go to Upminster and see the busy town."

"Upminster," said she. "There I've never been. And what society is there? I must enquire."

"Men and women both," her husband said.

"Then," said she, "the respirator and the tulle, the gorgeous winceyette and kersey skirt."

"Have what you will," her husband said. "The folk are no doubt chic at Upminster."

"Then perhaps a jacquard silk," she said, "and tailored skirt of navy blue, the hat with birds, and a handbag with a single sequin and a golden clasp."

She put on her hat before the glass and dabbed the scented powder on her cheek.

"Neat and debonair," her husband said. "Now take my arm; we'll go."

Arm in arm they went, and stride by stride they strode; in a bus they rode, and then by underground.

"Such famous folks there'll be," said she, and smoothed her sleeve and hanked her hair.

At Upminster they looked about and walked the town. The shops were shut, the market closed, the sky was grey, and the clock had stopped.

"There's nothing here," said the London man.

"Indeed," said she. And they went home again.

Meat First, Grace Later

One time a woman, the widow of a huntsman, lived deep in a forest, a long way off, where the king would hunt, and she kept his lodge. But the king did not come, now that his huntsman was no longer there.

The woman had a big boy, Robin, and two little girls, Rose and Ruth. Her husband had died, so Robin had plenty of work to do, and it made him strong.

"It makes him a hard boy," said Rose; and Ruth said, "He will be a severe man."

"That is how I am," said Robin. "And now, Mother, what is there for supper?"

"I am boiling turnips in the pot," said their mother. "See them in the water. You may sleep for a while, and I shall wake you when they are ready."

So the children slept. But their mother had no turnips. She was boiling stones out of the field, because there was nothing else. She thought the children would not feel hunger if they slept.

There was a knock at the door, and an old man who had wandered in the forest came begging for food.

"We can give you no more than we have," said the mother.

"And not too much of that," said Robin, because he knew there was not much.

"But you may share our turnips," said Rose and Ruth.

"Then tell your mother to look in the pot," said the old man.

"No, not that," said the mother. "There is nothing in it but stones out of the field." But when she took the lid from the pot it was full of beans, dumplings and sausages.

"I thought I came to the right house," said the old man. The mother could say nothing. She thought she was dreaming. She served out the meal and they were ready to start it.

"We give thanks for what we eat," said Rose, and Ruth said, "We ask a blessing on our meat."

But Robin said, "Meat first, Grace later."

"Is that the best you will say?" asked the old man.

"That's it," said Robin. "I'll have it safe inside first."

"I will say my Grace," said the old man, "and so will your mother. And my own little daughter I left behind me will say hers. You may eat now, Robin, but afterwards you will be changed three times, and until you can say your Grace you will stay changed."

"I could say something now, I dare say," said Robin. "If I wished."

"Not now," said the old man, and it was so. Robin could say nothing. With his mouth he could only eat, and even that was hard. Then he dropped his spoon and fell from his stool, and could not stand up like a man, because he had changed into a deer, and went running out of the door into the night, as if the hunt had started after him.

"Is it a bad thing you have done to him?" asked his sisters.

"No," said the old man. "He will do well enough, and he may say his Grace at any time and change again."

When they had finished eating the old man went away, and after that, each day, there was food in the pot for the mother and her two daughters.

On each of those days the girls would go into the forest and often found the deer that was Robin beside a stream. They would put their arms about him and place a garland round his neck, and bring him leaves to eat. But he would not say grace first.

One day the garland had gone, and in its place was a fine silky golden cord, but Robin could not speak and tell them why it came.

One day, after a year had passed, they found Robin as a boy once more, and they were very joyful.

"We have brought you bread," said Rose; and Ruth said, "We have brought you milk."

"I shall eat the bread," said Robin, "and drink the milk."

"But will you say Grace first?" asked Rose.

"No," said Robin. "In the forest we eat first and say Grace later, because while we bend our heads to graze or lift them to browse, the bear, or wolf, or hunter will come upon us, and what good is our blessing to us then?"

So he ate the bread, and tasted the milk, and there, before the eyes of his sisters he began to grow scales and turned to a golden fish, and dropped down into the river and swam away.

His sisters and his mother wept and wept, because he was too hard in his heart to say Grace and come back to them.

Far away, on the other side of the forest, at London's Tower, a princess was weeping too, because there never came back to her the wild deer she loved, to eat from her hand and let her draw him by the golden silky cord she made from her own hair to capture him.

Rose and Ruth and their mother did not know of her. Each day they came down to the stream and waited for the fish. Some days he would come to them, and take crumbs of bread from their hands.

Far off in the city beyond the forest the princess almost forgot the deer and loved instead the great golden fish that would come to the bank of the Thames for her. One day she let down a golden hook to catch him by and take him home, but the line, made of a single one of her hairs, broke, and the hook stayed in the fish's mouth.

When a year had gone by the fish rose from the water in front of his sisters and said, "I do not want those little crumbs of bread now; I want full pieces."

Robin was a boy again, and once more they were joyful. But he still would not say Grace when they brought him bread and new white wine.

"It is meat first in the water," he said. "It is no good saying Grace if what you bite hides a hook like the one in my throat now. It is all watch, and eat, and lucky to live."

He bit his bread, and dropped it on the ground, and bent to peck at it, because this time he had changed into a raven. He took the bread and flew off with it, and said, "Kah," and not any Grace at all.

But each day he would come to his sisters, until the winter was on the forest, and he no longer came. Each day too, he saw the princess, who wept for her fish, thinking it had been taken by a fisherman.

In the winter Robin the raven came to the king's palace, in at a window where there was a table full of things to eat; and without saying Grace he began taking what he wanted. One of the serving men put a silver dish-cover over him and brought him to the king.

"Did he say Grace?" asked the king.

"Not a word of it," said the serving man.

"His neck must be wrung," said the king. "Perhaps."

"No," said the princess. "He followed me home, so do not take his life, because he knows no better. I shall put a gold ring on his leg, and gold chain to the ring, and I shall keep him."

"Very well," said the king. "And when the winter is over you must let him go again."

Now the raven was always with the princess, and she loved him and talked to him, and he said, "Kah", back to her.

"You can do better than that," said the princess.

"Kah," said Robin. And then he thought, I wish I were a boy again and could speak, because though I love this princess I should dearly like to visit my little sisters and my mother. They will not know what has become of me.

He thought then that perhaps he should say his Grace and be changed back. But he could only say "Kah", no matter what he thought. Perhaps he did not think enough at first.

One day the princess said, "My father the king says that you may not come to table until you say your Grace, so now say it: 'We give thanks before we eat'."

"Kah," said Robin, and it was all he could do.

"You are a difficult bird, I think," said the princess. "And you do not love me, or you would speak the Grace."

"Kah," said Robin, and it was his only word. But he could not come to the king's table until he knew his Grace.

So he tried, and then he could say, "Kah give kah for kah," and in a little while he could say, "We give kah for what we kah," and when he had tried a hundred times, or more, he could say it and he came to the table.

But still he would only say it after he had eaten, so he was sent away again.

When the winter was over, the princess, with tears in her eyes, took the gold chain from the gold ring on his leg, and let him go. He flew up to the ceiling, then down again through the halls of the palace to the table.

"We give thanks for what we eat," he said, alone among the dishes, "we ask a blessing on our meat," and then he began his breakfast.

He had at last said Grace before meat, and began to change into a boy again. At once he remembered his mother and sisters and ran from the room and out of the palace.

When the princess found he was gone she thought he had flown, and was very sorry she had undone the gold chain. The king said, "We shall find him: I think I know where he is."

Laying aside his crown, and walking alone like any man, he led the princess into the forest, and far away to the woman's lodge.

The mother and the girls, and Robin, saw him coming when they were in the middle of their joy. To them he was the old beggar man again, and they came to greet him. Then they understood that he was the king, who had come looking for a good young man for his daughter, and chosen Robin, though he would not say Grace before meat at that time.

But the princess said, "I may not love him. I have loved enough, first a deer, then a golden fish, then a raven, and now they have all gone away I shall never love again."

When she had said this she saw on Robin's finger the gold ring she had put on the raven's leg, and she took from his mouth the gold hook the fish had swallowed, and she found on his neck the cord of her own hair she had put round the neck of the deer.

"Oh," she said, "I have loved three times the same thing, so to love again is the same again," and she was joyful, and so was Robin.

"Now he is not a hard boy," said Rose; and Ruth said, "Nor yet a severe man."

So they all came to the Tower, which was the palace, and the princess was like a sister to the two girls, and like a daughter to their mother.

After that, when Robin had married the princess, all of them would come far out into the forest, to the lodge there, and eat from the pot that was always full.

If you find it, half a day's walk west from London Tower, in the great hunting park, why there you shall eat from it, with your Grace first, meat later. Or as you please, if you have listened long enough to know.

ᘒ Barnaby's Dream ᘒ

A plain man was Barnaby when he set out from home to walk a day and a night and a day and a night, once and again and again, to London City.

"'Tis plain," he said, as he stumped through the countryside, "that I shall get a wage and a dry place in all the city streets, and fare better than in the straw at home."

Because at home, somewhere back of Bristol, where he started from, there was only the weather and the farms, the ploughing and the harvest.

"Plain I may be," said Barnaby, "but I know I be better than all that old country work."

He had two gold coins in his pocket and rich as a king he felt. But plain is sensible, and he showed them to no one. He had the rind of a cheese and the crust of a loaf, and drank the rain that fell on him.

"Until I come to London," he said. "Then I'll be dry outside and wet within with cider."

He stumped the hard road and he chomped the hard rinds and champed the stiff crust and rattled his hard money a day or two more.

Then he smelt London, and it was rare and smoky; and he saw London, and it was dark and sour, and it was the other side of the river. On Barnaby's side there were some huts no country fellow would live in, and all the people working in the open in the rain, no better than in back of Bristol.

But just beyond there was a street of houses and shops, more than anything Barnaby had ever seen, and that street went right across the wide river to the other side, London Bridge with people living on it, and all London beyond.

"Well then, here I do be," said Barnaby. "Some parts do seem worse than home, and some parts too grand for I. So what be best for to do?"

And no one said, "How is the day, Barnaby?" for no one knew him; and no one smiled, because they hardly knew how; and when he spoke to them and said, "How bist thee?" they could not understand his ways of speaking, and he could not understand theirs.

But it would cost him four pennies to cross the bridge, and when he offered a gold coin they said it was made in the country and no good for city work.

"These do be the worst folks," said Barnaby out loud to himself, same as he might in a field with only birds to hear. Well, he was a plain man and said what he ought to say, whether they understood it or not.

They understood it, mind. They didn't have much to their names, but they had a ditch with all manner of dirty rubbish in it, and in a few minutes Barnaby was in it too, bruised and kicked.

A dog took his cheese rind; a screeching little girl took his crust; two scrounging boys took his two gold coins; and some more strong fellows searched him for the rest, but there wasn't anything else. Only plain Barnaby.

"I should have the law on they," said Barnaby. But the woman on the edge of the ditch laughed and asked him, "Who do you fink makes the laws round here? We do, ploughboy, we do."

Barnaby was in the ditch all day. When the day began to grow dark he crawled to the very end, and there was the river where he washed himself as clean as he might get.

"A hard life need not be a dirty one," he said, the same as his mother taught him. So he got clean. But he could not get himself away from the river except by climbing up into the ditch again.

"I shan't do that, plain as plain," he said. "I'll wait until it be not so dark."

So he sat, cold and wet, hungry and thirsty, robbed and poor, and shivered under the first archway.

Over and above him there were houses and dinners frying and folk talking. They might have been kindly, he thought, and he called out. A window opened, but only for a cobblestone to splash in the mud beside him and a voice to tell him to be off.

"I be as off as I can get," said Barnaby. But he thought it best not to call out again.

All grew quiet on the bridge and under it, and beyond the river the light of the city died down, and its noise. Only the cries of the night-watchmen could be heard across the water.

"This be none of I," said Barnaby to himself. "But I did

plainly set out for London, and to London I shall be just so soon as I can see."

He did not have time to work on the matter, because then, in all the quiet cold night, he heard some very little voice calling out piteously not far off.

On top of his shivers Barnaby felt all his spine prickle. "I don't care for that," he said, with his teeth all a-rattle.

And the little voice cried on and cried on, like nothing Barnaby ever heard day or night Bristol way. "Nobody heard such as that," he told himself. "Hold your peace, now," he told the little voice, and shut his eyes and blocked his ears.

And he didn't like to look, and he did wish to, and in the end he did. "For there be a plain account to be made of everything," he said, "and I be the man for that." That's what he told himself, without believing it.

And he looked, and there was a little bluish ghosty light down against the arch wall, flicker and wink, come and go, and out of it the crying.

Barnaby was a plain man, and those were plain times. Once a man would have made a sign of the cross, or said a holy name. But Barnaby did none of that. He watched and he listened.

Because there was another voice, and another light, high up the wall of the arch, calling and crying too, the light greenish and spirity.

"I plain don't believe," said Barnaby, though he saw it plainly there and heard it too, like a fallen nestling, and likely to be some city bird too grand for the country.

"Now then, what's your trouble?" he said. "A man can't sleep for noise."

There was a shuddery silence for a bit, and the lights down dim. But up they come again, mournful, tearing at Barnaby's heart so doleful they were.

So far he had come to no harm. He got down on his knees by the wall foot and looked at what might be there. "I'll be tender to the little bird," he said. He could not think it was anything else. "Just a little beak," he said, "for such a little noise."

He saw what was there. It had two legs. Like a bird. It had two wings, bedrabbled with mud. Like a bird. It hadn't a beak like a bird. It had a little sweet face like a pretty child, all dawbed with tears and blushed by crying.

"It be a little maid of whatever sort," said Barnaby. "It be a dear little maid, and it do have fallen from its nest, that be plain, and the mother do be calling from above and not a soul do come to help she."

He looked up and he saw a mother one of the same kind, and she dared fly down now, but durst not land in the muds and slime by the riverside.

It was worse than that too, with the tide coming up the Thames and the water lapping close to the arch wall.

"Now my pretties," said Barnaby, because they were so fair they stole his senses, "mother, you do let I pick she up and bring she to thee, but in my big hands, I do feel ashamed of they, too big for town and best manning a plough or a cart." This be the fairies, he said to himself. Up to town is where they all got to, for I never saw one before.

He knew what to do, whatever the creatures were.

He edged the little one on to his finger end and then on his great palm, and lifted it up to the mother. She lived where there was a brick out of the work, and hauled her little one off Barnaby's hand, dosed it with a slap, and set it down safe, and shook her head to Barnaby. He knew she meant it was a naughty baby, but what can you do these days? and thank you, kind gentleman.

"'Tis nothing, truly," said Barnaby. But for all that he felt as if he did a whole day's work all at once, which was strange from lifting something with no weight at all. "And at least it be peaceful."

It might be peaceful. But now his feet were standing in water, because the tide had come up so fast, and came faster too, over his knees, and to his waist, and lifting him so that he had to hold on to the bricks of the arch to stay where he was.

"In the end," he said, "I'll wash upstream or downstream and I shan't never get to the further side, or London, or a dry place and a wage, and I wish I never set out from the country."

However, while he wished that, he found the little mother creature was holding his arm and pulling him in at the place where she lived. Big as he was, he was small enough too to come in there, and go up a cracky way through the brickwork into the dry and the warm.

And here there was a fire going, and little pots of ale offered, though he would have preferred cider. He drank what was to take, and he ate bread as white as clouds, and warmed himself. And fell dreadfully and plainly in love with the little fairy mother, while knowing she would dance on his hand if he truly woke up.

Then the fairy women went away and only the men were left. Barnaby thought his heart broke straight through, but there was no time for that. The men were setting off on a hunt, and Barnaby was to go with them.

They rode on rats. "Big as cart-horses they are," said Barnaby to himself. "What's after giddy-up?"

The hunt came next. It hunted cats. It went under floors, through walls, across beds, into cupboards, down wells, up drains, around rooftops, all the length of London Bridge.

And they ran the cats out of town. "'Tis like a dream," said Barnaby, all worn out with riding and hallooing. "Now to be back with that pretty lady and her shining wings, oh, I do love she."

But the hunt went home without him. His rat slid away out of its bridle, and the saddle was a dry leaf. Barnaby was sitting inside the city gate, across the bridge and where he wanted to be.

Instead of a torn shirt and ripped breeches he had on a gown of fur and good wool cloth on his legs, a warm cap on his head, and a pocket with something in it.

"My gold coins," he said, bringing them out and laying

them on that big palm. There they were still when his pocket rattled once more, and he pulled out another two gold coins beside the first.

"Well, I don't believe," he said, and dropped the coins back in again.

Then a man came by and bowed, and asked his pleasure, and brought a coach for him to ride in, and Barnaby understood none of this.

"I'd sooner be back with the fairy lady," he said. But people round him would have none of that. Into the coach he had to get, and round the streets with people cheering. Hurrah, they said, for Sir Barnaby Bright, come to London seven years since and already Lord Mayor, hurrah, God bless us all.

Barnaby was too plain for all this. He sat where he was, longing for his pretty fairy lady, and hearing money rattle in his pocket. And when he took out the six gold coins, another six grew in their place, so that he had to throw the money out of the window to be rid of the weight.

He supposed it must be true. "Or I wouldn't be to here," he said. "Seven years hunting cats, or seven years supping fairy ale. I don't know, but the plain fact be that I be where I be."

The ride was over at a great house, and there to meet him was the lady mayoress and five pretty children. And if it was a dream who would want to wake up? Because this was the same pretty fairy lady out of the bridge, and her children, all too shy and modest to let their wings be seen.

And for all that, plain Barnaby will now and then sit by his fireside and wish he had a cart to load with straw, or a plough to lay another furrow, in the back of beyond Bristol.

ᗡᕐ *Thieving Martin* ᕐᗡ

Hanging Thieving Martin on the elm tree at Tyburn was not easy in spite of all that he had done. His list of crimes started with being a highwayman on the Oxford Road (but only getting halfpence for his trouble from learned University Doctors who were above carrying money); melting down the silver from Abchurch in the City and finding it was only lead after all; poaching, cooking, and eating the Lord Mayor's white geese that were for the annual feast of the Redmaids' Charity and choking on the feathers which he was swallowing to stop them being found (the maids did not ever eat the geese, only the Trustees); claiming the pensions of four canons retired from St Paul's and spending it on windmills for the choirboys, then selling the choirboys as slaves down on the river and going back for the canons (the slave owners complained about the canons and that's what got Thieving Martin caught); selling forty gallons of ink to the tax collectors without telling them it was the invisible sort and wiping out all their records; picking the pockets of an angler and going home to his wife and dog with all his takings and she finding they were all worms and maggots, so Thieving Martin went to steal a cow at Smithfield Market, lost his way, and came back with an elephant which wouldn't go through the door, so they had to move because it was so obvious; unwinding Big Ben until it ran backwards into yesterday and Thieving Martin could claim another free Sunday dinner; taking the train to Brighton and leaving it there (this was very early on in the Railway Age) so that everyone had to walk home; going fishing in winter and bringing back a whole frozen pond and opening an unplanned skating rink and selling fried tadpoles (both these things being entirely against the law); refusing to pay his gas bill and taking to the office all the gas he had used and claiming his money back; charging people money to get out of the zoo, but all the rich animals got out first and the people had to stay; starting a law case against the government for hiding one of the country's suns, which started a war with the French when they thought we had two and had never told them; burying his head in the sand and making people pay to hear it talk and all it ever said was, "Put another penny in"; inventing the donkey without due care and attention; drawing white lines on the snow so that Wimbledon was a shambles; and then blaming it all on the dog.

He was probably right, though: the highly respectable clergyman who out of pity attended the hanging, being asked by Thieving Martin to look after his talking dog Chesterfield, was walking home with the downcast creature, when Chesterfield, muttering an apology, went off on his own for a few minutes; the reverend gentleman stayed at the same spot (a corner of Connaught Square) for five minutes, until the clever and well-brought-up canine returned and handed over a purse containing seven sovereigns, two half-crowns, a florin, and eleven pennies, a ticket to a prize-fight, and a telephone number, discovered three hundred years later to have been out of service, but the only clue to the owner of the purse; the dog served the old gentleman well in that manner for six years, but a month after he died (having accidentally swallowed a push-chair while stealing a set of valuable twins) the old gentleman was caught on all fours nibbling at the purse of a stout matron who was scratching his back, and sent to Battersea but was not deemed suitable for further training.

∞ 𝒫aying the Servant ∞

Xeng was the last Chinaman left in London once. All the rest had sailed away again, or died, and only Xeng kept house in a street along the Thames.

"One day another of my people will come," he said each day. "I have done nothing to deserve being lonely. Yet if that is my fortune, then I can bear it. But I am sure that one day I shall find a friend of my own race."

He kept on working, washing and ironing shirts for the sailors from the ships that came daily to the port of London.

Each time a customer came in Xeng would ask, "Have you been to my country? Have you brought back any of my people?"

"No, John," the sailors would say. "We've no trade there this time."

"But if you go," said Xeng, "tell them I am here and waiting for a word."

But he supposed that no sailor went to China, or if he did, that he forgot to hand on the message.

"From Shang-Hai, or Can-Ton, or Fragrant Harbour, surely the message would go to my father and my mother," Xeng told himself. "And if they are dead and have not told me, then my brothers and my sisters would send a message."

But the years went by, and no word went to China, and no word came back. Xeng grew older. He washed and ironed shirts more slowly with his frail hands. The sailors would come back for them at the end of the day and they would not be ironed.

Then more years passed, and the sailors would come and find the shirts had not been washed and dried.

Then at last the sailors did not come at all, because the house was too dirty and untidy, and it did not seem that anything could be clean in there, or made clean.

One day, though, there came a sailor who had many years since been to China, but who had only now got back to London, after going round the world ten times.

"My old mate John," he said. "It looks as if you are beyond laundering a shirt now, so I won't hand mine over. But I have something for you from one of your pigtailed relatives across the Yellow Sea."

He gave Xeng a box with some small things in.

"They said you might need some help," the sailor told Xeng. "But these days no one from that land is allowed to leave, and this was all that could come, so look after it well."

The sailor went back to his ship. Xeng looked at his little parcel for a long time.

"It is a present," he said. "No one owes me anything. But I must make my house tidy before I open the box."

He spent a day, and another day, and then he rested a day, before setting the box on the table and opening it.

Inside the box there was a sleeping rat, and beside it a large dragonfly from the Yang-tse River, also sleeping.

"It is a kindly gift, I am sure," said Xeng. "But I do not remember what it means."

However, there were words in the bottom of the box, and they read, "Bury us at the crossroads for three days, then we are joss-sticks."

"Almost I remember what it means," said Xeng.

He did as the writing said, and buried the sleeping rat and the sleeping dragonfly at the crossing of two paths.

Three days later he dug them up again. They now were like sticks of charcoal, but damp from the ground.

When they were dry he put them into his incense-burner. He had not been able to burn a joss-stick for many years, because no one in London made them.

He got an ember from his fire, and put the two creatures beside it, and hung the burner up.

Clouds of white smoke came out, and a smell of forests in the rain, and rivers in flood, and rice-fields ripening. Xeng was in tears at the memories.

In the morning something was moving in the incense-burner. Xeng brought it down, and from the ashes something jumped to the floor and began to run about.

Xeng knew what it was. He had seen one before, in China, but had not known where they came from.

"It is the greatest kindness," he said, "for my family to send me this in my greatest need."

The little thing on the floor was an elf, and it now had come to live with him. It was not really one thing only, but more like a nest of ants, a great many of it, but only known as one elf.

While it did not do much for him on purpose, it certainly kept the house perfectly clean and tidy, so that there was no dust from threshold to chimney-top.

And if there was laundry to be done it would do it, singing

all the time in an old language from before anything spoken in China today, or before anything ever spoken in London.

So Xeng was able to work again, and sailors again came with their shirts, and money began to be in his pocket once more.

So life got better for nearly a year. "John is looking himself again," his neighbours said, and the sailors were so pleased that sometimes he was given a plug of ship's tobacco to chew.

But when the year was coming to its end the elf spoke to him one day, and said, "The time is coming to pay me."

"I will pay you," said Xeng. "As much as I can. How much do you want?"

"Have I worked well?" asked the elf.

"Very well," said Xeng.

"Have I broken anything, or wasted anything, or torn or spoilt anything, or cost you anything?"

"Nothing at all," said Xeng. "You have made things all the better for me, and I am grateful to you for ever. Now, how much did you say you wanted?"

"You should remember what you pay an elf," said the elf.

"I have only heard the stories," said Xeng. "But that is not what you want."

In the stories the elf is paid by being given a man to eat each year.

"That is all I want," said the elf. "A man. I shall need him the day after tomorrow. And then I shall return to China and be a slave to no-one."

Xeng had forgotten that an elf need not be paid at once if he has broken or spoiled household goods, or caused a loss. By telling him there was no problem of that sort Xeng had acted foolishly.

"But I said I would pay," said Xeng, "and so I shall. The man will be sitting under the tree in the yard at dawn the day after tomorrow."

He knew what he had to do. He must not let the elf return to China and be a slave to no-one. If that happened it would eat up the land and all the people would be slaves to it.

Xeng gathered up the ashes from his incense-burner. He took his last silver Chinese coins from their safe place. He bundled the coins and the ashes together in a silk ribbon, and kept them ready for the right moment.

Just before dawn on the day for payment Xeng went out into the street and dropped the packet of silver coins there.

Then he returned to his yard and sat down under the tree to wait for dawn.

What happened to the silver coins, and the ash, and the elf, may be told somewhere else.

What happened to Xeng has already been told.

∾ *Fisherwoman* ∾

When the River Thames froze over in a long winter, the ice along the sea coast froze too. In one of those years a Finnwoman came down from the North along the ice in her skin boat. It seemed part of her because if ever she got out, she sewed herself in when she sat in it again. She was small and dark, and her eyes were deep-set and black

She got above London Bridge and settled on the ice. A good many folk were there already, and put up booths and binns and huts, and held a fair and markets and thievery of different sorts, from the eighth day of Christmas and into March, the frost holding so firm. She made herself a shelter of ice blocks, the first time such a thing was seen.

Some Scotchmen had come down with the King from their own country, and they knew her for what she was, a fairy of the sea. Her sort never left the water, they said. They paddle from Fair Isle to Orkney and all about, and can go swifter than a bird. The sailors say it is no luck at all to see one, and death to hear her speak.

The Finnwoman sawed a hole in the ice with a bone until she got to the water. Then she sat by and fished in it. No one saw her catch anything at all.

Nobody went to her, whatever the reason, and she went to

no one. But she could speak the London language, a bit after the Scotch fashion. Some boys threw stones at her, but she threw ice back, and they thought they had been witched because the next day they went through the ice below the bridge.

One day a merchant's wife, living just outside the Wall, sent her serving girl to the fair on the ice, to buy fish, if she could, for all their suppers. The girl went out not very pleased, wondering whether to spend the money and never come back.

She spent some time among the stalls of the market, without finding what she wanted, and that was making her peevish as well as disloyal. Then she came near the Finnwoman, and called out to her, for want of anyone better to cross.

"Why, Mother," she said, "with your feet in a sack" (because that was how the Finnwoman sat) "and fishing so idle, have you set a bait on your line?"

"I ha' done so," said the Finnwoman. "There's the fingers of sailors on there the now."

"I'll take the fish you catch," said the girl, and she was going on her way, the cold wind coming up through the arches of the bridge and her not wanting to wait. Since the Finnwoman had never caught a fish the girl was only teasing in her spiteful way.

But the Finnwoman there and then pulled up a great fish, knocked it on the head with the bone she used to cut ice, and slid it across to the servant girl.

And the girl, saying nothing, took the fish without offering to pay, because she was a cheat, and made it right with herself by having said she would take the fish.

So off she went, leaving the Finnwoman to call after her for money. Even a Finnwoman needs money in London. The girl laughed and wagged a finger, wrapped her arms round the fish, and went on her way.

"It will be fishes for you again tomorrow," said the Finnwoman. "Aye, that it will."

But this is easy, thought the girl, and kept the money she had been given by her mistress. She would leave service tomorrow, with twice as much in her pocket, she thought, and went back to the house.

She was well thanked when she got there, and the fish made a great meal for them all.

Only the girl herself could not fancy to eat it, saying she was cold and going to her bed. But the merchant and his wife and the children ate down to the bone on top, and in the kitchen the cook and the house-boys and the yardman and two clerks ate below the bone.

And in the morning each and every one was still at the table, stiff as death. The girl rose up and found them all like ice through, with their eyes open and all gazing at her.

She did not know what to do but run out of the house and on to the ice for company and to think what she could say if they brought her up for killing the household. And for filling her pockets with silver and good things, which she did before she left. And taking her breakfast with her, the length of a finger of the fish meat.

She kept away from the Finnwoman. But for all that she came upon her round the back of a canvas shop, and the little skin boat lying next to her. The girl was at that moment putting the finger–length of breakfast to her lips and tasting it.

"You come for your wee fishes, no doubt?" said the Finnwoman, but the girl had no such idea. However, it was too late, because she herself was at once stiff like the dead, only her eyes saw and saw as she swung about.

The Finnwoman pulled up her line, swung it round the girl's ankles, tripped her over, and the hole in the ice swallowed her up, just as she was, and her eyes turned white as if they were cooked.

The Finnwoman dropped ice into the hole and it sealed over, white as the girl's eyes. Then she took her bone and her skin boat to another part of the ice and cut another hole and began to fish again.

Before long she pulled out another long fish. It was just at this time of the day when word came down of the discovery at the merchant's house, of all the family and household stark and staring stiff around their last night's supper. Many of the crowd went to look, as people do. With them went the Finnwoman, on her short legs, carrying the fish.

The watchmen were there keeping order for the parish. But the Finnwoman did not leave as she was told, but would be in the house, and cooking her fish, no matter what they told her.

"Ogh, you will see," she told them, swilling out the fish-kettle and laying the fish in it, whole as it was. In a short time she had poached it until its eye was white, and when she had done that she set it on the merchant's table.

"Now," she told the beadle, "let them taste that. I will be off to Shetland again, now the ice is breaking." For the ice was moving by the bridge, and water begun to drip from eaves.

So she went from the house, and they could not stop her. The beadle took a finger-length of the fish and put it in the mouth of the merchant. At once the merchant blinked, sat up and spat, and on to the table fell a silver ornament that was a jewel for his wife.

The beadle took other portions for all the rest of the family round the table, and each one blinked and spat out coins or needle-cases or spoons, one after another, until all the family's precious goods lay before them.

Then they saw to the kitchen people and brought them back into the world, coughing and spluttering but not so full of precious things, the clerks with mouths full of ink, the house-boys shaking out lockets with their loves' name on.

But they well knew they were well rid of the girl, for each and every one had seen between them all the girl had stolen, through their own open eyes, and those were the very things returned.

That fish they finished, and they thought they never saw the girl again.

The Finnwoman sewed herself into her skin boat and skimmed herself away down the river and up the coast, fast as a bird, to the North again.

❧ *I Heard Something Crack* ❧

As I was going over London Bridge,
I heard something crack;
  Not a man in all England
Can mend that!

∽ Swanley Farm ∞

Building motorways causes problems to people that are not known to exist. If no one believes in you it is hard to be taken seriously, even if you are not ignored.

But some people in hard hats had to take notice of some farmers near Swanley, in Kent but joined to London. And it is London's M25 motorway that caused the problem, so this counts as a London story.

Near where Gildenhill Road overpasses the motorway there was a farm no one had seen. It was under the ground, so not very noticeable. Under the ground means a cave, so that had been noticed by the surveyors and builders, and they proposed to fill it with concrete, just like that. Because that was where the support of the overpass was to be, one leg on that spot, fixed and on the plans, and no problem to engineers.

They should have asked the farmers what they thought, instead of thinking they had a simple job. They should have asked people living near by about their neighbours. But there was no consultation, because, though the neighbours knew about these farmers, they simply didn't believe in them.

The contractors started by drilling a hole into the top of the cave, first thing one Monday morning. They had the drill, they had the pre–mix coming by the wagonload, and they had something worse too.

Jack Lee Geddes was the man using the drill, boring a shaft. It was a big thing on a tripod like an oil derrick or rig, making a hole about this much across. A dog might get down it, but not a man. The ground there was chalk and gault and greensand, and it wouldn't matter what it was with 720 diamonds ripping through it, and the water splashing out at the top streaked with mud, and Jack Lee Geddes looking at the colour to see how far down he'd got.

He knew to a minute when the water would be falling into the cave and not rising to the top again, and that was when to stop the drill and have a bit of peace from the engine while the core was hauled up. That's the pillar of rock that gets lifted out of the hole in two-metre lengths, and it goes off to the scientists.

Of course, the interesting bit was further down, in the cave, if you are an inquisitive type of person.

Jack Lee Geddes would have had his sandwiches while the core was being lifted. But that day he didn't quite feel like it.

There was a nasty smell, he told his foreman Billy Harlow. Billy said that maybe they'd gone through some limestone, which couldn't half smell of sulphur, mate.

Jack said it turned him up, and what's that noise, eh, Billy? Billy thought it was water down below, or maybe they'd struck oil and got rich for life. It stinks, does oil, he said. And makes noises.

Then the pre–mix was coming and the wagons waiting

and churning, like grinding their teeth, and the men chuntering because they got paid by the load not by how long it took.

But it did take a bit longer, because the men lifting the core began to turn their heads away from the job to stop breathing the smell. And then one by one they had to leave what they were doing and sit on the embankment and take deep breaths of fresh air. Then they began to feel rough and ill, and three of them heaved up their breakfasts.

It's bad, they said. It's the smell and it's the noise, and there's bad vibes.

Billy said that they could do vibes too, because they could, but not just yet. But in the meantime what are you getting paid for, you layabouts?

So they came back on the job, pale and sweaty, and got the core out and laid it on the bank ready to be taken away, twelve or more sections, smooth as marble.

The top of the hole was empty now, uncovered, ready for pouring. Jack Lee Geddes was going to lift a tundish into place, a sort of funnel to guide the concrete into the hole when the wagon came up with it. First, though he had to lower the vibrator, which shakes the mixture into every corner of a cavity.

The men were watching from a little way off because of the smell, or they would have been close by when things began to happen.

The vibrator went down on its thick black cable. Jack was rolling it from its trolley, about fifty-five feet of it to go. He hadn't got half of it, about, nine metres these days, fed through when . . .

Something took hold of the other end and pulled. The trolley fell over and was being dragged across the site. Jack went to rescue it, like instinct, but the men, standing a little way off, shouted at him to leave it.

They could see more than he could. They saw a sort of black air coming out of the hole, not smoke, not steam, but black air itself. You could smell it as well as see it.

Jack smelt it and came away. He had to. It gripped his throat like a living thing and wanted to stop him from breathing. So he was gasping and choking and slipping about on the thin clay.

And out of the hole came a hand. Something had not been pulling the cable but climbing up it, hand over hand.

So there was another hand. And then there was a head. And there was something sitting on the edge of the hole pulling the cable up, foot by foot, and throwing it back from where it sat in the black vapour.

There must have been twenty men watching, and they could never describe what they saw. Well, they could do it separately, but there was no way of getting their stories together. And none of them did anything useful. They all watched. Some said they were terrified, some said they were amazed, some said they must have died and Hell had come for them just as they expected.

Peggy Armitage, however, got out of her pre–mix wagon. She wasn't going to give in to things out of holes in the ground. She took a good look at the thing, decided against it, and just at the moment it pulled the business end of the vibrator into its two hands, she stepped across to the switch and turned it on.

She was brave, but was she sensible? She only wanted the thing out of the way and her mix poured ready to collect another for another part of the site, money in her pocket.

The thing became very unhappy at once. It did not like the way things were going, and it knew who had set them off. Of course it was the government really, deciding on a motorway just there, but it had an eye on Peggy Armitage's wagon sitting there throbbing gently as it magimixed its gravel and cement.

It did not let go of the vibrator, though its teeth were chattering. It gripped that firmly, let out a screech, and walked in its slopping low-slung way across to Peggy's wagon, and vibrated that. It shoved the vibrator through the radiator, and all the greenish water ran out.

The vibration of the engine and the vibration of the vibrator began to chime together, thud, chonk, thud, chonk, bang, bang, bang, until the wagon was jumping on its springs, and then on its wheels, and then sheerly off the ground. The vat of concrete began to swing and come loose. It tipped, and poured itself, and the container fell off.

The cab came off the wagon. The wheels loosened themselves and rolled away. The steering wheel spun into the air and lodged in the top of the drill rig.

You might think of turning off the vibrator, but no one there felt inclined to do it. They all backed off. Because not only was the creature from the hole still stamping about, and turning its attention to the rig itself, but another hand, and another, began to emerge from the hole, and more breaths of choking air billowed out ahead of another creature like the first.

Peggy Armitage was furious with the men for not doing

anything. She was furious with herself for having done anything. Goblins, she was saying, I know goblins when I see them.

Billy was saying, We should have come to an arrangement, you know, talked to them. There were tales before we got here, down in Swanley and Hextable. But you can't take notice of everything.

The goblins, if that is what they were, were certainly talking to each other. First there were two, and then more came up out of the ground. They were all plainly cross, and if the contractor's men blamed one another for what had gone wrong, the goblins blamed each other too, and there was plenty of quarrelling.

Not just goblins came out. Some of them brought out farming things, like scythes and reaphooks and hayrakes and wheelbarrows. And then a cartwheel made of a curly fossil, and another, and all four, and the cart itself in pieces, and put together.

Jack Lee Geddes said it was clever.

It was disgusting, said Billy Harlow. And then up they dragged a little horse, tugging it out and getting it on its feet and putting it in the shafts of the cart.

They piled the cart with underground hay made from roots. On top of that they put household gear like stony tables and baskets made of chalk, and their babies like maggots. And then another cart came up, and goblin dogs and white underground sheep with wispy coats, and blind geese.

All this time the first goblin was waving the vibrator like a sword, and there wasn't a man would face him. And it wasn't made better by the goblin holding his snout (it wasn't quite a nose) as if the men smelt worse than goblins.

Well, I don't know, said Peggy Armitage, each to his own taste I say, and got round behind and turned the vibrator off again.

By this time the goblin farmers were ready to leave. But they had nowhere to go, so they stood in the rain along the hedge side, and looked that unhappy you could cry if you saw them.

Well lads, said Billy, looking the other way, we've had a long lay-off, but we'd best get the job done and the hole filled.

But Peggy Armitage could only wonder how to explain what happened to her wagon. Someone would want to know.

Skidded on the slippery clay, Jack Lee Geddes told her, we all saw it happen, hit the rig, and rolled over, lucky to get out alive, girl.

That was true, Peggy said.

Right, we'll pour, said Jack.

And they poured, and they vibrated, and the mix filled the cave, and rose up the hole, and the job was done.

At the end of all that there were the goblins, not stirred from the spot, wringing wet, and washed clean by rain. When the lads were moving off the first one of them came across to look down the hole again, wanting to be away down it and home.

There was no hole there. It was all plugged with concrete, and a spike of iron standing in it to join it to the north-east column of the overpass, down beside the slow lane of the clockwise M25.

So he went back and told the others, and there they were all shivering, goblins, babies, sheep, the weasely thing like a dog, the bristly thing like a cat. Each and every one staring at the men, at Jack Lee Geddes, at Billy Harlow, at Peggy Armitage.

They aren't there, said Peggy.

They are, said Billy. We can't walk away.

I have to, said Peggy, see what they did with my truck. But she didn't walk off. She couldn't.

There's the geology plans, said Jack Lee Geddes, just in the hut and I'll get them. He had something in mind. Hang about, he said, we can maybe do something.

The cave they had filled was not the only one marked. In the next field over there was another, much bigger, about the same depth below ground.

Come on lads, we've got the equipment so let's shift it, said Jack. And all the drivers got hold of the drilling derrick and lifted it over the fence in among the stuff growing there, cabbages and so on, and put it in the right place.

They drilled out another hole, about fifty feet deep. And when they had taken the core out they listened down it, and all was quiet and smelling fresh.

The next bit is my job, said Peggy. She went to the goblins and held out a hand. It took a long time for the chief goblin to hold his out. He didn't want another buzz like the last one. She led him across between the wet cabbages and showed him the hole.

He looked down it, and he sniffed it, and he tried a toe in it. Then he went back for the next goblin, and they had a look together. But they weren't going down it just like that.

They took one of their dogs and put him down, like poachers sending a ferret in, very like it in fact. In a little while the dog got to the bottom and seemed to be looking round. Then it clambered out and wagged its pointed tail.

Then a goblin lad was sent down, and he was soon squealing away at the bottom, but it was good news. Before long the carts were in pieces again and being taken down, and all the babies and the goblin people.

There was just one problem. The chief one wanted to put a big flat stone over the hole, but when he did he couldn't get down the hole, and couldn't work out how to fix it.

I'll do it, said Jack Lee Geddes. You go down and I'll put it on top. And then the little goblin went in again, but he was out at once with something in his hand, and that was for Peggy, because of what happened to her pre–mix wagon.

Jack put the stone over the hole, buried it with earth, and they left the cabbage patch.

Peggy took the stone home. It was flint, carved like a spearhead, and she always said it was lucky for her. And there, under the field by Gildenhill Road, is the underground farm. To this day there's a smell of goblins if you stand at the foot of the north-east column of the overpass.

⁂ *Dick Whittington* ⁂

Dick Whittington was a paw-about idle jock of a boy that never did a good day's work without a clouted ear, never wrote a page at school without a welted bottom, and never let a girl alone without he got soused in the pond by her father or her brothers.

So it was always that tomorrow would see him better done by, and the week after his own master; but it wasn't that way, because he could keep no master, there was no pretty girl he did not offend; and at last he was sent from his own home for loafing about in such a dinder all day long and eating his weight in the week. And, the countryside was tired of him and knew he would be in trouble and they would have to pay.

So he had nowhere to go, and no friends of the same temper, so nowhere is where he went, out on the road to see where it led and there and back to see how far it was.

There was a little house cat following him, and he threw a pebble or two at it but it didn't notice, only followed him on and on mewing and playing with a leaf, like Dick waiting for something to turn up.

The day's end turned up. Darkness came on. Dick thought they would surely call for him, but no one did. They would have to if they wanted him, because he had no idea of the way home, and it was no good following the cat because it was following him.

So he sat under a tree that night, and the cat climbed on his lap and they were both hungry. They were hungry a day or two more, out between the villages, lost as sheep and dry as dust.

They got a crust and a crumb at a village, but got sent on their way at daylight, and a smart walk to the next place, and so on.

Then the villages got bigger and closer to each other, and at last they all ran together and were called London, outside the city wall and inside it.

But there was nothing to eat for the asking, and little for the taking. Only the little cat fattened on mice, which she brought to Dick, but he could not eat them, or he would have taken them.

It was the cat that saved him. One day she went into a yard at the back of a merchant's house, and was busy with her claws and teeth, and had six or seven mice laid out dead. Dick was picking them up, wondering if he might sell them. He still had no sense.

He had them by the tails when the merchant came from the house. Even Dick did not have enough free cheek to ask him to buy mice, so he kept still, just chirping to the cat to come by and they would be out of this place. But the merchant, Mr Fitzwarren, came straight to him first, and counted the mice, and said, "That's seven. Here's sixpence for them."

"Here you are then, sir," said Dick, taking the money with one hand and with the other holding the mice up for Mr Fitzwarren to take.

"No," said Mr Fitzwarren, putting the money in his hand, "you must be rid of them yourself, now you have caught them. Of course I do not want them."

So off he went, and Dick was left with money and mice, and then the cat as well. And this was his best wages for his least work. He had not been so idle as this even when he was at home in a frock.

He thought he might do it again. So he picked up the cat and went to another merchant's yard, and took sevenpence this time, and threepence at another, and six at a third. But then he ran into Mr Fitzwarren again at a fourth house.

Mr Fitzwarren did not give him any more money. Instead, he took Dick by the ear and took him back to his own house, and Dick thought he would be beaten for sure.

"Don't hurt the cat," he said. "She never thought of it."

"No, you did," said Mr Fitzwarren. "But it was a good trick, and if I hadn't seen your cat from my own window catching them I'd be wanting my sixpence back. Now, good tricks are worth something to a merchant, so now you belong to me, and so do all your tricks."

Dick was given a room at Mr Fitzwarren's house, told to wash himself at the pump, and be at the counting-house with the cat at seven the next morning.

There he was made to count and write, and he would sooner have had a beating. He was made to work and stay awake, and he would rather have been lost along the road again. He was made to listen to stories about the merchant's business with the kings of Africa and India.

And it wasn't like him. If the merchant's daughter Alice had not been there, neither would Dick. But there she was, in and out of the counting-house and not seeing Dick at all, though he sighed and spoke and gazed at her. But each time she came she looked once his way and not again.

The first time he saw her his quill pen scratched the page. The second time its new-cut nib crossed itself and made a blot. The third time he spilt his horn of ink.

So for her he stayed and worked, until Mr Fitzwarren began to think he knew something. Dick did not care what Mr Fitzwarren thought, if only Alice would.

Then Alice went out to the country somewhere to visit her aunt, and it was said she might not trouble to return. Dick began to yawn now, and to come in late, and to turn in faulty work. The chief clerk said he would be turned out, but Dick did not care.

The next day he did not get up. The day after that he did, but only to cross the yard to the street and set off for Nowhere again, with the cat.

And so he went. But when he got to the edge of the heath overlooking London he turned round and sat on a milestone to look at the city below, just as the churches were to start Evensong.

All the bells were ringing, and all the bells were ringing the same message quite clear:

Turn again, Whittington,
Lord Mayor of London.

So the little cat thought she would go back, with or without Dick. And Dick thought he would go back, because someone had to care for the cat.

And lucky it was that the day he did not work was a holiday Saturday, and the next one a Sunday. On Monday he went to the counting-house, and waited for Tuesday.

Tuesday did not come to him in the counting house, because on Monday Mr Fitzwarren told him to go down to the docks next morning and join a ship sailing to the Indies.

"You are to run the trade from her," Mr Fitzwarren said. "We are dealing with the Barbarines, and you can be as artful as they are."

So Dick went down to the docks, with the little cat following, and sailed for the Indies with the little cat as well.

When they got to the kingdom of the Barbarines they were called to the palace for their dinner.

"This is where the trading begins," said the captain. "Mr Fitzwarren says that you will have a trick or two up your sleeve."

"Oh, I have only the cat," said Dick, because there she was, in a sort of nest, seeing the new country and wanting her share of dinner. She was getting very fat.

It was a sad business at the palace, where the Barbarines sat round a dirty and empty table, and there was nothing to eat.

"Oh, we cannot tell you," said the king of the Barbarines, "and we do not know the name, because such a thing has not happened before. You will leave us in disgust when you hear, but please do not mock."

So he told them that out of the desert just beyond had come a swarm like a carpet of small animals that went everywhere, ate everything, and could not be caught because they ran and hid so fast.

"Just a minute," said the cat, coming out of Dick's sleeve. "Don't go away, because this sounds like my sort of problem. Mice." Well, that is what Dick told the king she had said, because at once she ran to a corner of the room and brought back two mice. One she ate, the other she killed and gave to the king. She was wonderfully thin now.

"It is wonderful," said the king. And the cat went under the table and brought out four more mice, killed dead.

"We shall buy this house-lion," said the king. "Bring a bag of money."

"Not so hasty," said Dick. "We have the same problems at home, and what could we do without our little lions?"

So they came and they went with bags of gold. The captain thought Dick would sell the cat when the money got high and the jewels were shining. But Dick had his hand in his sleeve.

"I am just finding the price of a cat," he said. "We shall make ten times as much."

Because in his sleeve he had felt and counted ten kittens, born that very moment, waiting for their mother to come back.

The ship stayed in that country for two months, while the kittens grew enough to leave their mother. And for each one they got ten bags of money and jewels.

"Mr Fitzwarren will be pleased," said the captain.

However, Mr Fitzwarren was not pleased, because Dick said the money was all his. "You did not send the cat," said Dick. "I took that, and I sold my kittens and the king bought them from me and I shall keep the money."

But of course there was an arrangement to be made, as usual, and they made it. It was quite simple, and quite fair, and Mr Fitzwarren was happy, Dick was happy, and Alice was happy too. Now she was able to notice a rich young merchant, if she couldn't bring herself to it before.

"But I always looked," she said. "But if I looked more than once I would blush and my secret be known."

Because Dick let Mr Fitzwarren have half the treasure, kept half himself, and set up as a merchant in the City of London, with Alice by his side for ever and a wedding under a church that played his tune over again.

And when it was his turn, and in the time of Henry the Fifth, he was Lord Mayor, Sir Richard Whittington, two or three times, like a litter.

ᗢ𝓗ere Sits the Lord Mayor ᗢ

Here sits the Lord Mayor,
Here sits his two men,
    Here sits the cock,
And here sits the hen.
    Here sits the chickens,
And here they go in,
    Chippety,
            chippety,
                    chippety,
                            chin.

∽ *The Cup of Wine* ∽

Hadrian, the Emperor of Rome, was in London on business early in the second century. He enjoyed travel very much, but many people thought he should have stayed in Rome all the time.

I tell you all this in confidence, mind. No gossip should go about.

At a meeting in a council room of the Tower of London some of his advisors were talking about this to him. They sat round the table with cups of wine, and the candles flickered in the wind.

"No," he said, "Rome is the Empire, the Empire is Rome. We are all Roman citizens, even that troublesome fellow Paul from Tarsus, talking about this new religion. So I am here in London to see about building a wall to keep out people from Scotland who will certainly never qualify as citizens of anywhere."

Not all the advisors were faithful to Hadrian. It is not always possible to tell who has turned against you and might want to be Emperor instead.

So the Emperor has his testers and his tasters as well as his bodyguard.

Out in the room beyond the faithful servants of the

Emperor, and the faithful servants of the advisors made ready the food and the drink, or brought logs through for the fire.

"Twenty feet high," Hadrian was saying. "And from coast to coast it will lie. Build it on rock where there is rock. Put a fort every mile, and a watch-post between the forts. Put gateways in it, with a trap behind, and let the wild tattooed men from Caledonia bring their sheep and goats and fire-water drink for sale. If they act up, chop off their heads."

In all this he was speaking wisely, because the Empire and Rome are more than any pagan tribe.

"Och," one of the servants was saying in the room beyond, "wait until the Campbells and the Macdonalds and the MacGregors and the Menzies and the Stewarts all get together, and we will wipe off the face of the earth this little city of Rome and all the Empire, and we shall extend our kingdom, as far south as Birmingham, maybe."

This was wee man, or parvulus, who washed in fire-water, oh, every year, and cleaned his throat with it many times a day. Otherwise he would not have spoken out loud.

But no one could understand his version of Latin.

He was waiting for his master Callitexus to speak. He had been waiting ever since the Emperor Hadrian landed at Deal and marched up to London. Callitexus was a Latin romantic novelist who thought Caledonia would be a fun place.

The parvulus was waiting for the order to pour a certain something from a particular bottle, or ampulla, into the Emperor's cup.

And when the Emperor died from drinking it, Callitexus would seize Britain, and perhaps the whole Empire, and the

Caledonians would ride south, probably on their goats, and that would be that for ever.

The sooner the better, the parvulus thought. This is a gey cauld tower where we live the now.

Of course it was not used often, because this was the first time for a hundred years the Emperor had visited Britain. It had not been dusted since the time of Julius Caesar.

And then the signal came. Callitexus had heard enough about the new wall to keep his friends out. It was time to slay Hadrian. He sent the order through to the serving room.

"A wee dram to round it off," said the parvulus, and got out the ampulla, and drew the cork. He poured the contents into Hadrian's cup, and carried it through himself.

And went back to wait for the Emperor to die. He had his instructions then, to deal with the other servants, and support Callitexus while he rode for the crown.

But there was only a shout of laughter from the council room. And Callitexus came through from there carrying a cup.

He set it down on the table. "We are discovered," he said. "Hadrian has found out. He has sent the poisoned cup back."

He drew out his sword and fell on it, and lay there dead.

"Poisoned?" said another servant. "By Callitexus?"

And the parvulus looked into the cup. How should Hadrian know it was poisoned? Had he magic?

The parvulus understood when he looked. Not for the last time had a small creature decided the fate of Caledonia. In the dark wine there struggled a spider, fallen from the rafters above. And it was for that the Emperor had sent it away.

"It is nothing," said another servant and, picking up the cup, he drank it off, spider and all.

They all thought the spider had killed him. But the parvulus knew.

He had no sword, being only slightly better than a slave. So he got a good large skewer from the kitchen and fell on that.

"Where is my wine?" called Hadrian, and went on with his work. "There should be a wide ditch on our side, and a road all the way along. Of course we shall charge VAT on everything that come to the markets by the gates. At the ends by the seas we should have lighthouses. I expect it will only be a temporary structure . . ."

Only you and I know all the details of this matter.

⊙ King Arthur at the Tower ⊙

King Arthur, in his time, ruled all the land of Britain and was king in London too. "By Trow and Tray and Kingdom Come I'll rule and be the master of my home," he said.

And knights and maidens heard his boastly cry, but from down below the Tower came a call.

 "I'll rule," said Arthur, "I'll rule both bold and tender now the land is clear of foes." In castle and in garth they heard him speak and nothing against him thought.

But down below the Tower something moved and cried again.

Arthur digged with sword and gavelock, with mattock and with hoe, between the stones, below the turf, where in the hill something lived and moved and probably had disagreed.

A day and night did Arthur dig below the Tower wall, and red-legged blackbirds of the sea came down to watch. And the ships tied up where the tree-trunks mark the water's edge.

"This is for a man's thirst," said Arthur when the sun

arose again and he was dry and they brought him cider from the apples of Avalon.

"And who shall drink it?" said the voice within the Tower hill.

"It is my Kingdom," Arthur said. "I'll drink it first and thou shalt dangle dry."

Then the red-legged birds flew into a tree and watched, with no more to say.

Arthur found what he was digging for, a head that looked at him, its nostrils breathing, and its speaking mouth.

"I'm King," says Arthur. "I'm in charge and keep the realm."

"I'm more," says the head. "I'm here now that was here before."

"I am and I was and I shall be," says Arthur.

And the head shouted so that the ground shook and the ships were cast loose when the river wall took up its stumps of tree and walked away. It shouted, "I shall be before you were, I was before you shall be. You are a man."

"Thou art a head," said Arthur, because there was no man below it, only chalk and clay.

"The head rules the weather and the harbour," said the head. "It is not known whether my body is flesh or fish."

"It is a crayfish," said Arthur. "You shall join it in the bottom of the river."

But with that the head sent the birds away with a flirt of his eyebrow.

"Bring them back," said Arthur, because they had not gone for ever.

"Now your luck is gone too," said the head. "What have you done, ruler of men?"

"I shall cut you off," said Arthur. But the head laughed because that had been done and made no difference. The body still slept at Caer Beddwyr. "My knights will cut you off," said Arthur.

"They have no power," said the head. "Only over men. I am before men. I am a god. I am the head of a god. If I were the least toe of a god, that is still more than you."

"There is something that cut you from your body," said Arthur. "Whatever you are you are not the greatest."

"I am Bran," said the head. "I am under the Tower to watch London and keep it from harm.

"I do that," said Arthur. "A man's work."

"They are my sea-ravens with red legs," said Bran. "If they go they do not come back."

"I shall say farewell," said Arthur. And the sea-ravens flew and have never been to the Tower again.

Arthur later called in the black ravens, and they are there to this day. But they are a sign of a lost battle.

"And I have taken your ships' landing place," said Bran. "Those are my alder trees that made it. Can your tree last so long?"

Arthur called for oak from the great tree that made his round table. But oak shall pass away, and elm will rot, and only alder stands the salt tide and the sweet.

"And now," said Bran, and bit Arthur on the foot.

"It is nothing," said Arthur.

Bran bit him at the ankle.

"It is less," cried Arthur.

Bran bit him on the calf.

"I near felt that," Arthur shouted.

Bran bit his knee.

"I'll not go lame," Arthur told him.

Bran bit him on the thigh.

"Ticklesome," cried Arthur.

Bran made to bite again. But Arthur leapt from the hole. "What next?" he said. "Let a man alone."

"Let a god alone," said Bran. "You rule man and country and I'll rule the world below and watch for those beyond. It is why I was set here. Let me alone."

"Aye, so let it be," said Arthur. "But no longer shall you bite me up and up my leg."

With sword and hand and plough Arthur buried Bran again to keep the realm in safety free.

But sea-ravens came there none, and the landing place was washed clear away by the sea.

∽ *The Waits* ∽

One Christmas-tide, when snow was on the city wall, and ice hung on the eaves, the Company of City Waits gathered to sing.

"Tonight," the Song Master said, "this Christmas Eve, we go in order to the Guildhall, and show ourselves a worthy company, both woman, man and child, sing our songs, and act our parts."

"We'll come and go together," his wife the Mistress said, "cause no offence, and offer worthy merchants no excuse to keep from us our pay."

"Conduct yourselves well," the Master said, "and we shall walk the streets with no fear of Prentice Boys, or Beggars from the ditch."

"Nor even," said his daughter Armigil to her brother Mace, "be afraid of wolves from the forest who come in the city gates by night."

"Hush," her mother said. "Your fancy is untrue."

But Armigil was sure, and Mace was certain that he knew, and held his sister's hand.

"Now we practise all our season's songs," the master said, "Christmas and its Twelve Days. Strike up with 'Holly is the Softest Bed'."

They sang that, and 'The Song of Visiting Kings', the carol

of 'The Baby Most Wise', the story of 'Herod and the Sheep', and 'The Litany of God's Mothe'r, which made them all weep.

"And now," said Armigil's mother to her, "put on a clean kirtle and your tippet with the silver fur. Mace shall wash his hands and face and wear his bonnet stitched from squares of silk."

"It is the very grandest day," said Mace. "You must call me Thomas, because it is indeed my name."

"We shall call you Mace," said Armigil. "Or dirty face." So he went to wash as he was told.

The Waits fetched out their instruments of music, their sheets of tunes, their papers full of words. The Master lit the lanterns, the Mistress opened up the door, and they stepped into the black night.

"Cold," said one to another, and clapped their hands; and the church bell struck for six o'clock.

"Hasten before the cold locks our voices and our tunes," said the Mistress. "Go quiet, and ignore the Prentice Lads or any vagabonds."

Off they went like shadows in the shadows of the night. Somewhere the Prentice Boys were at their wicked songs; and down beside the river the Ditch Beggars quarrelled over rags and bones.

Now Mace's face was clean, his hands were dry. "Hurry, hurry, hurry," said his sister Armigil. When they came to the house door, the street before was empty, the room behind unoccupied. The Waits had gone without them, quiet as they were told.

"Mother," called Armigil, and heard no reply.

"Papa?" said Mace, but no one heard. A cold wind

brought the songs of Prentice Boys along the street, the shouts of Beggars from the ditch.

"We know where Guildhall is," said Armigil. "We'll catch them up."

"Never say how we were left at home," said Mace.

"That would be indeed the worst of any trouble," said Armigil. "As we go we'll sing a song we have rehearsed, 'The Litany of God's Mother'." She pulled close her tippet of the silver fur, and began a little song, while Mace held tight her hand, his cap of silken squares hard on his head.

At the first corner they stopped to see the way, all in the

dark. There were few lamps in those streets, and none to show the way across.

"We take this side, I think," said Armigil. "I wish I better knew the road." She sang a word or two of litany, and then stopped and stood.

"Amen," said Mace, because it was that time.

"Prentice Boys are coming near," said Armigil.

"I'll fight," said Mace.

"And the Ditch Beggars are inside the City gate," said Armigil. "Look small and be not seen."

"I hear them shout," said Mace. All around shutters went up on house and shop, doors were barred, lights were doused, and the City darker still.

"I'll sing," said Armigil, and sang another line.

And all at once they heard a strange reply, like the litany, unlike it too, and yet the same.

"It is this way," said Armigil. "I heard."

"I heard it too," said Mace. "It is not Prentice Boys, nor Beggars, nor the Company of Waits."

"So beautiful," said Armigil, "that we are safe."

The Prentice Boys sang closer now. Ditch Beggars thumped staves upon the cobbles and shouted back.

"They go to fight each other," said Mace. "I should like to watch, indeed I would."

And, naughty boy, he ran away along the street. Armigil called after him, but he had gone. The shouting song of Prentice Boys came round a corner.

From another came the Beggars from the ditch.

The Prentice Boys had flaming torches to light them on their way. The Beggars burnt fatty bones like candles.

Between the Beggars and the Prentices stood Mace, but not like a ragged boy they would not notice, in his better breeches, and the silken cap, all gleaming in the light of torch and bone.

"Hi," cried the Prentice Boys, all shrill.

"Ho," called the Beggars, harsh and deep.

"Mace," called Armigil, but no one heard.

"Armigil," Mace called out, but where she was he could not tell.

"I cannot look," said Armigil, alone and in the dark. "Mace is lost, and it is my fault."

But Mace had run a different way. Prentice Boys and the Beggars ran to chase him.

"The cap," the Beggars called, "we'll throw him in the

river, and keep it as a prize."

"No," the Prentice Boys were promising, "we'll burn the cap and barbecue the boy, to teach him not to parade our streets."

Off they ran, out of sight and soon out of sound.

"What will they do?" said Armigil. "I am not yet near the Guildhall, and I have lost a brother and a Wait." She sang another little verse of litany.

And again, inside the silent City, something like a reply came on the cold wind. A verse was answering, so like her song, but yet so strange.

It was all there was. No people walked the streets, no lights showed. The moon was muffled behind a cloud.

Armigil sang again. Again there was a song upon the air, not quite in key, but sweet and comforting.

"What it is I do not know," said Armigil. "Or where; but I shall go that way."

She went along the street under houses high and dark with night. Far away Prentice Boys and Beggars were chasing Mace. She heard their shouts and screams.

From the City gate she heard another sound. Forest wolves were running along the City ways.

Far ahead she thought she saw a light, a house with open door and fire within. When she sang to keep her spirits up, the other tune replied.

"It is the Guildhall I can see," she said. "The Waits are singing as they should, but the song is changed along the street by echoes and the wind. I'll hurry on, and tell them what became of Mace; and that indeed it is not my fault."

She heard the wolves behind, to one side the Prentice Boys, to the other Ditch Beggars running. And Mace was there ahead of her, not knowing where to go, but still with his cap upon his head.

"Mace," called Armigil. "Stay there. I am coming. We are saved and at the Guildhall."

"No," called Mace, "It is not that place. Look behind you at the wolves."

The wolves were sniffing at her heels.

"And to one hand," said Mace; and Prentice Boys were crowding in that street. "And the other;" and Ditch Beggars filled an alley.

"This is richer goods," called a Prentice Boy. "A fur tippet."

"That is a lady," called the Beggars. "She shall live in the Ditch with us."

They were on three sides of Armigil, and only Mace to help her, who was saying, like a brother, "It is all your fault."

Armigil thought she now must die. "I will say my prayers first," she said. "That is right."

"It is the law," said the Beggars.

"The law not help," said the Prentice Boys.

The wolves howled, but waited too.

Armigil could remember nothing of any prayer. Not a word came to her. "I shall go straight to the bad place," she told herself. "I shall just sing more of the song." And she sang another verse of 'The Litany of God's Mother'.

"Is that all?" the Prentice Boys shouted, when she had stopped. But they were not so fierce.

"There is another verse," said Armigil, and she sang another.

She thought Mace joined in with her, but she was not sure. She heard another voice, that was all.

"We have not listened to such songs," said the Ditch Beggars. And they seemed nearly friendly. "Sing more," they said. "See what will save you."

Armigil sang again. This time the light along the street grew brighter, and there was singing from it, and the sound of instruments.

"Ah," said the Prentice Boys.

"Oh," said the Ditch Beggars.

And the wolves sat down and wagged their tails.

"Look," said Mace. He had turned and seen the bright light. There was more singing coming from that place.

"It is the Company of Waits," said Armigil.

"You have tricked us," said the Prentice Boys.

"Throw them all in the river," growled the Ditch Beggars.

And the wolves snarled.

The light grew very bright, and then very clear. In the City street itself there stood a stable, with straw, and a manger holding a Baby, Mary sitting beside it, Joseph standing by and singing 'Holly is the Softest Bed'.

Then Mary came out on to the City street, as if she lived close by, and called forward the Ditch Beggars.

"You shall be the kings for now, and not be outcast while you are," she said. So the Ditch Beggars sang 'The Song of Visiting Kings', as if they wore robes and crowns instead of rags.

Then Mary summoned the Prentice Boys. "You must learn pity and faith," she said, and told them to sing 'Herod and the Sheep', where Herod learns he has done wrong.

During these songs wolves came and watched over the manger, and tried to sing 'The Baby Most Wise', but had to be helped with the words and the tune.

Then Mary and Armigil sang 'The Litany of God's Mother'. The Prentice Boys stole away, singing it, and the Ditch Beggars carried the song back to their ditch. The wolves went to the forest again.

Mace went off alone. But at the end of the song, when the stable had gone back into darkness with Mary and Joseph and Baby, he came back, leading his father, the Master of the Company of Waits, and his mother, their Mistress, and the Waits themselves.

They found Armigil sitting on a doorstep, singing the end of the Litany to herself, by herself.

"So, Madam All-Alone," said her mother. "You have missed your way and seen nothing."

"Oh no," said Armigil. "I have been talking to such people and singing with them."

"So have we," said her father, "and done well without you, and hold up our heads in pride."

"We saw the Prentice Boys, and the Ditch Beggars, the Holy Family, and the wolves," said Armigil. "Didn't we, Mace?"

"Yes," said Mace.

"Oh, Thomas," said his mother, "the cold weather and that bright cap have gone to your head. Come away home and be done with your nonsense."

"We know," said Mace.

Armigil took his hand. "We know," she said.

The Master led them home, all singing 'Holly is the Softest Bed'.

∞ *The Wooden Goose* ∞

Once there was a big lake that used to lie where Wanstead Flats now are. One Christmas-time there, neither voice nor visitor came to disturb Ranulf the woodcarver. Only his own family ran about beside the house by day, and clamoured in it by night for something to eat.

"We are truly out of the way of all mankind," said Ranulf to his four little sons and his three baby daughters.

"Christmas has forgotten the likes of us," said Editha, his wife. "Now, is there some kindling better than wet peat from the lake-shore to draw up the fire?"

"What is fire," said Ranulf, "with nothing to cook upon it? We have neither money nor food, and Christmas would not know us if it came through the roof at once."

But Editha looked in her stone larder and found a bone that would boil for broth, and barley to thicken it. "And there is the shell of a cheese," she said. "So draw up the fire, Ranulf, draw it to boil and then simmer."

But there was only the wet peat, and no tree in sight for many years now, so the fire lived in a small way in its hearth. There was more smoke than flame, and faint hope indeed of boiling the pot.

And all the while Ranulf thought about the next thing he

would carve. "It is to be my last," he said. "There is no more to say. Let it be standing here within the house when they find our bones in the spring." And he stroked the bough he had carried from the peat bog, where old oak is found.

He did not know what he should make of it, until it was begun and finished. No man knows what is in the future. But he had kept that bough for a full seven years, drying it and thinking what it might hold in its grain.

But Editha said, "Its past is long enough. I know the future of that wood, Ranulf. The future of it is in the fire this Christmas night."

Ranulf shook his head. "I alone know what it shall be," he said. "And not yet; only when I have finished forming it with knife and shave. My hand and my eye are not ready."

"You will hear another story," said Editha, "if you let your hand feel the chill upon these children of yours; let your eye rest upon the bones that are coming through their pale skin. Is there something better on your mind than warming and feeding them?"

"No, indeed," said Ranulf. "The time is close when I shall make a marvel from that wood, and someone will buy it at the market. Then we shall be rich for a time."

His sons looked at him with round eyes, his daughters beseeched him to feed them, and Editha held the soup pot on the miserable fire.

"You see what market there is for your skill," she said, meaning that there was none here.

"I do," said Ranulf. With a heavy heart he took his axe and his saw and split the beam of bog-oak from end to end, twice and thrice and more. Then he sawed the lengths and laid them on the fire.

But the one piece he kept, that he could not split, that he could not saw. It was the great knot at the base of the branch, and it was like stone. He laid it aside as if it were a stone, and of no use.

Then the flames began to eat what was given them, for the fire was hungry and cold too. Its new heat began to boil the pot, so that out of the bacon bone and the barley and some few leaves from the hillside and the lakeside, there came the smell of food as the gravy thickened.

Now the pain of waiting was greatest. If there is nothing to expect your mouth does not water; and if your mouth does not water your stomach does not weep.

So they waited, until towards night the barley was soft and the pleasure had come from the bone and flavoured the whole pot.

"Where there is smell there is taste," said Editha. "Now we are ready to take a little each, and carry some warmth to bed with us."

Only Ranulf stood back, wondering what he should make of the knot of wood, and whether he could do what was asked of him.

"For I do not know when I begin what I am to do," he said to himself. "I can only be ready to do it, cost what it may."

Before they could eat there came a noise along the lakeshore, which was the jangling of bits and bridles, and the sighing of horses, and the talk of men.

In the last light of the day their metal shone softly, at the pommel of their saddles, at the hilt of their swords, and on every bronze fitting of their harness. Brightest of all it shone upon jewels they wore at their throats.

All Ranulf's young things came out to look at them as they rode the margin of the water. Hunger was a commonplace to them, but armoured men on horses were a rare sight, and very welcome.

Or that was so at first. The riders saw the pale faces waiting in the twilight, and stopped beside the hut.

"We will have refreshment," said their leader. "We have ridden all the hours of the day."

"And the night is yet to come," said another.

"Which will be colder yet," said the third and last.

Their horses shuffled their hooves in the gravel of the strand, and the little waves of the lake ran back and forth among them.

"So bring out some food," said the leader. "We have come upon you at the best time, and I smell some broth."

"We have but little," said Editha. "It was for the childer, see how many there are, and how starved they are."

"They are here for the next meal," said the leader of the horsemen, "when we shall be far from any house. So bring out what you have."

All three of them flashed swords from their scabbards, and the edges grated sharp on the last flame of sunset.

Editha could only do what she was told. She brought the pot from the fire and handed it up. The leader took it and drank from it.

"Poor enough," he said. "If that is the best you can offer, small wonder that your children do not prosper. You should be ashamed, woman."

"We eat what there is," said Ranulf. "Nothing more comes our way."

"We have come your way," said the leading horseman,

"and that is an honour for you."

Ranulf said nothing. He had no idea who the riders were, and whether it was glorious to meet them, or not. The second rider took some broth, and handed the pot to the third.

"It is vile," he said, and, "It is like poison," said the third. He threw the pot into the lake and the little waves closed over it.

"Small thanks for your kindness," said the leader. "We shall go on our way." All three gathered up their reins and rode on.

Editha stood and watched them until they could be seen no more.

"They have gone," said one of the small sons, at last.

"They have not gone," said Editha. "They came to stay for ever. Those three are death, because we now shall die, and we are without hope. There is nothing left for us in this world, and little in the next. We have made no mark on the world, and it forgets us."

Ranulf sat against the house wall, where the thatch did not quite touch the ground. "I am ashamed again," he told himself. "I dared not speak against those swords. I was defeated by their sharp edges. Editha is right, and those men have been the death of us."

He sat and he wondered. Inside the hut the fire went out and the hearth was cold. Outside it Ranulf was wakeful all night with the only things he had in the world beyond his family. These things were the burins and scrapers, the rasps and the knives he used for carving wood.

The one last piece of wood lay on his knees, with his hands upon it wondering what was in the wood, feeling the weight and the lie of the grain.

Dark or light, day or night, the hands tell the carver all he knows. So in the night Ranulf's hands worked on their own, as they should. The time had come for them to do so, and the time for Ranulf to see what he had done did not come during the darkness. He did not know what he had carved.

"It is our memorial," he said. "This is Ranulf and Editha and their seven children, dead at Christmas. This is all we have left, a scrap of useless wood, and our few years together."

There came a time when he laid down his tools, and felt with his hands that the carving was complete. He did not know yet what it was. He waited for daylight, and it was slow coming.

"Perhaps we shall die before it comes," he said. "We do not want to look forward to our last day. Let us have had it already."

He went to sleep, thinking he would not wake again. He did not see that his hands fell away from the carving so that it stood there free. He did not hear how it ruffled its feathers and stretched its neck. He did not know that it spread its wings and lifted itself into the air and flew away, leaving only a wooden goose-quill on the grass.

But as it went it called, and inside the little house the children heard the call and woke to the morning. They came out and saw the sun making the lake golden. They saw their father sitting against the wall with his tools.

"See what he has made us," they called. But there was nothing beside Ranulf beyond a heap of wood shavings and the dust from his work. As for himself, they were not sure he was alive, so deep was his sleep.

"There is nothing," said Editha. "Let him sleep. We shall be together again soon. We are for leaving this world."

"We shall go anywhere that has pudding," said the children.

"There will be banquets," said Editha. "That is it."

From across the lake there flew a bird. It came over the water and over the strand, and settled on the roof of the house, upon the thatch, beside the hole where smoke rose when there was a fire.

The bird called, and walked about. Ranulf heard the voice of it, and knew what it was. He woke and looked.

He knew now what he had carved. He saw a goose walking and heard it calling. He had thought of it perhaps, as he carved, and made something fit for a Christmas dinner. But at the same time he thought this was a dream, because no wooden goose could make a dinner.

"I will catch it," he said, all the same. "We shall dine."

"But no," said his eldest son. "It is not a bird to eat. This bird is golden."

"It is green," said a sister.

"It is the colour of nightingales," said Editha.

"No," said another son, "it is red and with a long tail that hangs down."

And another said it was white, with yellow legs.

"It is a dream only," said Ranulf. "So I will not catch it. Why, in real life it is only wood, if it is anything."

All the same, they all watched the bird so intently that they did not see what followed it across the lake.

There were four boats, suddenly, their keels grating on the shore. Out of them stepped nine men and nine ladies, and nine hounds, and the last boat was empty.

So all at once there were many people beside the hut. And each one of them also saw a different bird upon the roof.

"It is indeed a dream," said Ranulf. "We have died."

But they had not. When Ranulf knew in his senses that the bird was truly only a wooden goose, and the chief of the nine men and the chief of the nine women had declared the same, then Ranulf knew who his visitors were.

"Your Majesty has come upon us at a bad time," he said. "We have neither fire nor food, and it was unworthy of me to carve a wooden goose in the dark. We are about to die, so you should leave us."

But it was not like that. It was more than that. The wooden goose had flown to the palace of the king of the Angles, in its round walls, and walked and called on the pointed roof. It had woken the king, and then flown back across the lake. The king had wished to know what made this thing, and followed with the chief people of the court.

So, by the end of the day, the fourth boat was filled with the family of Ranulf, making another nine people, and they went back to the palace and into a round house. But before they slept there was a feast, and Christmas came that time.

There Ranulf and Editha and the seven children lived. But the wooden goose, that had flown and called, neither called nor flew again.

"Such things come at need," said Ranulf. "But I hope we have no such need in the time to come."

But he wonders, often, whether it is still all a dream, or they have come to heaven.

Only on that lake, when it forms again, will that bird alight again.

∽ My Little Dawkins ∽

Goosefair Day is round the first of November in All Saints' Churchyard in Stratford. Men and girls bring geese to sell for the London poultrymen to fatten on for Christmas.

Martha was a simple-hearted girl from some simple-hearted place like Geslingthorpe. She had one gander of her own that she loved more than all the young men, but not so much as she loved her little brothers and sisters. She called him My Little Dawkins. He would put his head in her lap and be her pet, and she would scratch at his neck.

"That won't fatten him," said her mother, and Martha would tell her not to say that, because the gander had to go and money come back to keep the little ones; because it is the city folk who eat the fat geese, not the country folk that have raised them.

Instead of letting him go down with a flock from the rest of the parish Martha was sure she had to take him herself.

"Then I shan't be cheated on the road," she said, "or at the Goosefair." But she meant she would be the longer with her pet, My Little Dawkins. As well as that, she longed to see the rich city of London and bring back a trinket or a memory.

"Then always manage for yourself," her mother advised. "Help does not ever come free." She gave Martha a silver penny in case she needed it.

Like all the other gooseherds Martha shod My Little Dawkins by tarring his feet, and she put a little red ribbon on his leg, to know him again.

With her goose-stick and her bonnet she set off with the other flocks, leading My Little Dawkins on a string, keeping him and herself apart from the rest.

"For you never know," she said. "Not all geese have been brought up gentle and proper; and tender and firm." Then she would drop a little tear for My Little Dawkins, who would get his head chopped off near Christmas. "Well," she thought, "it might be the Lord Mayor, and him send for me to cook the dinner."

She didn't think that if it was so, My Little Dawkins would be that dinner.

Well, love is where love is, we can't help it if it makes us foolish. But it is best not to talk of it.

The first night she built her own little fire, and sat round it with her flock of one but never was she so far from home before, and did not know the memory of that would lag with her so sharp.

The next night she sat for company by the flockmaster's fire with the other gooseherds. One of the herding lads sat alongside her, but she spoke to no one and nothing but My Little Dawkins.

"There now, Martha, you need a man to help you drive," said that herding lad.

"My Little Dawkins is man enough for me," said Martha. Mind you, she thought the herding lad was as pretty as anyone she had met. But she turned away and dropped a tear, and another because she was cold and the way was long, and she did miss her little brothers and sisters so.

In a day or two more she wondered whether My Little Dawkins was prospering, and fancied he had grown thinner.

"Great thieves in this county," said the herding lad, when she at last spoke to him, just to ask whether it was always so.

"Why, what do you mean?" she asked.

"One goose is like another," said the herding lad.

"But this is My Little Dawkins," said Martha. "See, he has a red ribbon on his leg." My Little Dawkins knew her well and would talk to her, but no one knew the meaning of all his gobble.

He pecked at that boy until he went away.

"'Tis you yourself," said Martha to My Little Dawkins. "Who else?"

"A goose is a goose," said the lad.

A morning or so later My Little Dawkins was but skin and bone. Gone was all the fat and meat that should nearly trail to the ground.

"But you grazed plenty on the way," said Martha, and gave him her own bread to help him, and went hungry.

"Being such a man for you has tuckered him all out," said the lad. "Is he still enough?"

"I'll thank you to look after your own," said Martha, and the lad went back to his own flock.

Before the week was out My Little Dawkins had grown smaller in himself, and his head did not reach so high, and he was not so loving any more.

"He knows what you have in mind for him," said the

herding lad. "He won't be worth buying for fattening. Why not walk with me, and that would bring you along proper?"

But Martha shook her head, and My Little Dawkins turned his away from her.

When London smoke was on the air My Little Dawkins had grown a grey feather.

When All Saints' Church came in sight his wings were grey across, like the wild birds. My Little Dawkins pecked at Martha, and hissed at her, and his eye was staring.

"I don't know that I love you still," said Martha. "But I can't bear not to, and I don't know what has got into you, for you are not the same bird I hatched against my own warm body."

My Little Dawkins tried to fly away, but the cord was round his neck.

"He never was like this," said Martha.

"You should have let me help," said the herding boy. "Take or leave."

"Help does not ever come free," said Martha. The herding lad was a pretty boy, but love is where love is, even if My Little Dawkins was so changed and otherly.

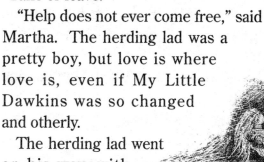

The herding lad went on his way, with the fine fat healthy geese of his that he was sure to sell.

It was just as he said. The poulterers came by, and they came by, and not one of them would look at My Little Dawkins, wild and grey.

There Martha was, alone with him at the end of the day, that should have had money to live on, with a trinket in her apron pocket for the little ones; and now there was to be none of that but empty-handed return.

"There is nothing for me," she said, when she sat on a tombstone in the churchyard with My Little Dawkins beside her. "If I go home I shall not take enough to help them through the winter, so I might as well not go."

And she sobbed now, thinking that her life was nearly over and nothing had come of it and all the pleasures she had looked forward to were lost.

"Oh, My Little Dawkins," she said, putting her arms about his neck, "I might just as well let you go free to fly the world and live as let them kill and eat you, for they won't do that even, and I am sorry to have brought you at all."

She loosed the cord from his neck, and he flew on to a tomb and on a wall and on a roof and to the tower of the church, and off he went.

"So that's all gone," said Martha. "And I am not to walk home, for what good am I."

The herding lad looked at her and laughed unkindly. "A simpleton like you should bide at home with your own foolish family," he said. "I did well enough, but you shall not share."

Then he went off, counting his money.

Martha thought that if she had been kinder to him the lad would have helped. But that was over.

She did not go home. She stayed at Stratford while she

had the silver penny still, and then walked to the city of London. She thought she was miserable before, but when the city gates were closed and she was inside she had no home to go to. She was taken up as a beggar and locked in the jail.

She was not happy, but next to the jail was something that made matters not so bad. There was a yard there full of geese, being fattened for Christmas. They were each eating daily more than a prisoner was given in a week. She looked at them, and they looked at her. She spoke goose-talk to them, and they gabbled and hissed to her behind the barred window.

"I suppose it be worse for you," she said. "I am not bound to die and be eaten in a few weeks. I truly wish we could all escape."

The next day one of the geese brought her a beak full of barley, which they were fed on. It went back for another, and another, until Martha had enough to live on, and day after day after that it brought beakfuls four and five times.

"But you are not My Little Dawkins," said Martha, because this goose was strong and white and well plumped out, and besides had no red ribbon on its leg.

Martha began to see how foolish she had been. When this goose talked with her it sounded like My Little Dawkins, because he had always spoken just as all geese do, never a word different.

Then Christmas was to hand, and the geese were being taken away. The poultryman came in to take away the best-fleshed, and white feathers drifted in the wind.

But still Martha was brought grain night and morning. At last only one goose was left, because it had grown too

skinny for the trade. This was the one that had given its
grain to Martha.

On the night before Christmas, when the bells were
ringing, and the frost came in, Martha thought the cold
would kill her. But the jailer came and sent her out into the
street, because at this season the jail must be empty, and the
people of the city could feed her or send her away, because
he did not care.

The poultryman, at that moment too, released the last
skinny goose. Martha met it at the corner and they walked
out of the city.

"Nobody wants us," she said, and sat down on a milestone
on the road towards Stratford, because she thought she
would start home and at least tell them why she had died.

The goose put his head in her lap, and she scratched his
neck, and knew that he was her own My Little Dawkins.

My Little Dawkins spoke to her then in words she
understood.

"The herding boy stole me," he said. "And put a worse
goose in my place, and did it again and again, hoping that
you would come to him, and you never did."

"Help does not ever come free, my mother said," Martha
told him.

"She is right," said My Little Dawkins. "You have
scratched my head, and see, I am fat again." He had
thickened out and was covered in soft flesh. "And I have
eaten better than barley. Now you must take and kill me,
and bring me to the best door in the city of London."

The world does not know the pain for her of cutting off
My Little Dawkins's head. But he twitched his legs, and
that was that, and she had a goose to sell.

Early in the morning, when the gates of London were open again, she went through and found the greatest door inside, carrying the poor dead My Little Dawkins, and tears were on her face.

This was the door of the Lord Mayor, and behind it there was great trouble, because, with one thing and another, neither cook nor mistress had been to market to buy the Christmas goose, and the maid had gone home, and there was neither service nor dinner for the Lord Mayor, and the house was in turmoil.

So the mistress bought the goose and the cook took Martha for a kitchen-maid, where it was warm by the great roasting fire.

Martha's first duty was to prepare the goose. She had to pluck the feathers off, and then use the knife. She well knew how to remove the giblets.

She found how My Little Dawkins had eaten better than barley, because in his throat was a silver coin, in his gullet was a golden coin, and behind his heart there was a ring with a precious stone.

Martha put them in her own pocket, because that was what My Little Dawkins meant her to do. And the mistress paid her for the goose, and for her work.

And in the deep snows she came to her own door at Geslingthorpe.

"I took no help," she said. "But I paid all the same," and gave her brothers and sisters all that she had gained.

The herding boy is still walking to London for Christmas.

∞ *Wheat from Danzig* ∞

People were once very rich at Tilbury Docks, bringing in all the goods from other lands by ship, and looking after the King's Navy too.

Wealth made them very proud and hard, and the wealthiest and the hardest and the proudest of them all was a widow who had lost her merchant husband in a shipwreck and kept on the business and ran it herself, which was not commonly done in those days. She was a hard mistress to deal with.

One day she said to the captain of her greatest ship, "Set sail at once, Captain, and bring me back a large cargo of the most precious thing in the world."

The captain did not understand her very well. "I cannot read your mind, ma'am," he said. "Do you require Chinese silks, gold from the Indies, jewels, slaves, the wood of unknown trees?"

"I leave that to you," replied the lady. "I wish to outshine and dazzle all the town of London, not just Tilbury. Your voyage is to find out the most highly valued thing in the world, and bring me a large cargo of it, as much as you can. No one is to know before you leave what you are bringing. You have served me well so far; let me see what you do now."

That captain thought that if he pleased her greatly he might come to marry her and share her life, and bring her back to her simple senses.

So he went to his ship. When it had sailed out of sight of land he called his officers, and told them what his mistress had ordered him to do.

"But what," he said, "is the most precious thing in the world?"

"Gold," said the first mate.

"Fine silks," said the second.

"Diamonds," said another.

And so it went round, with apes and ivory and wine being mentioned.

But the little cabin-boy thought something else, which the rest had forgotten. He said, "I have known what it is like to be without food, because now I eat it three and four times a day, but not always when I was a child. So the greatest thing is often a crust of bread."

The captain saw that he spoke the truth. "Steer to the north," he said, "past Denmark and into the Baltic Sea and to the town of Danzig."

At Danzig he filled his holds with wheat, and put out on the return voyage.

Meanwhile the merchant's widow had not been able to keep silent. She let the rich townspeople of Tilbury and London know that she had sent her captain to bring a cargo of the most precious thing to be found in the world.

"She will come down with a bump," the people said. "She has got above herself."

In a few days the captain came back, and the people said, when they saw his ship coming upriver, "Well, he has failed.

He will be in trouble."

"How quick you have been!" the widow told the captain. "What have you brought me?"

"A large cargo of the finest Danzig wheat," said the captain. "That is what we decided upon, and we are proud of our choice."

"Wheat? Common wheat that grows in fields everywhere?" the widow shouted. " I asked for the most precious thing in the world and you bring me some vulgar, ordinary, common wheat! That will impress no one, and is of no value. Before you are dismissed from my service for ever, throw the whole cargo into the sea."

And, in spite of the poor in Tilbury and London, and needy beggars and captives, the captain had to do as he was told.

But before he did so he told the widow that the day would come when she knew hunger herself, and would think of the good wheat cast away.

The widow told him to leave, taking no notice, knowing she was among the richest people in Tilbury.

But when she reached her house a great storm began to rage, and some days afterwards she received news that her other ships had been destroyed, and she began to have no trade and no money coming in.

In the same tempest a great bar of sand was thrown up just down the river from Tilbury, on the edge of Walton Common. The very ship full of wheat was wrecked before the cargo was put out of it, and buried in the sandbank. And that was the last of the widow's hopes. She now had no ships.

For some months she managed to live by selling her

jewels, and then her furniture. But when the spring came all her money was gone. She went to her rich friends and begged for food, but they were glad to see her in trouble and only gave her scraps at the back door. They too were feeling less rich, because the same bank of sand had filled the haven and harbour at Tilbury and no ships could put in.

One morning in April, as the widow was passing by and looking at the sandbank, hoping to find anything of value or fit to eat, she saw that it was covered with small green stems, fine as hair.

The wheat from the wrecked ship had sprouted in the mud on the sandbank, and was now growing richly.

By now she knew when to speak and when not to, when to boast and when to be humble. Like the cabin-boy, she knew what hunger was. So now she waited until the wheat was ripe and then told the people of Tilbury that they could take the crop.

But she was not a trader for nothing, and the next year after she farmed the sands herself, and the year after that married the captain, and settled down into a sensible way of life.

∞ *The Proud Tailor* ∞

There was a tailor in Cheapside who sewed a fine seam enough and had a nimble needle. He had a nimble tongue too, and his clients would come to see how their suits were finishing, and stay to pass the time of day.

Then they would go to their counting-houses or places of office and send on all the comical and laughing sayings of the tailor.

Then more merchants and lawyers would come and order their suits, and stay to talk and listen.

After a year or two of this the tailor became rather vain, and thought himself quite a wit, and that men stayed to hear his wisdom. But for the most part they heard him make a fool of himself by not understanding the world at all, and they were not laughing with him but at him.

However, the tailor thought he was quite the court of wisdom and that the world nodded when he did, and that at the courts of law and seat of government his words were taken as the best opinion.

And he began to get ideas above his station.

"I cannot have these common bent and weary spoons about me," he said to his cleaning lady, who did her very best.

"I do what I can," she said. "I can't do more."

"Nor can I any longer have these worn knives to my table," he said to himself. "And these forks with but three or four tines, they quite will not do. If the Lord Chief Justice should come for breeches to wear to Parliament and he came into the house, if he did me such an honour, and he is likely to, I should have to use something better, both for serving his lordship, and also for making in the kitchen anything that was to pass his lips."

"Lawks, how you do go, Mr Lapel, sir," said his cleaning lady.

He thought he went on very well and that the cleaning lady was disrespectful. So he told her not to come to the house any more, and she never did.

The knives and the forks and the spoons had done well enough for the tailor's father, and thought they were worthy still, and made of silver, though they had been cleaned thin over the years. Before long, now there was no cleaning lady, they were black through no fault of their own.

"If we could choose," they told each other, "we should choose someone who cares."

So a fork stabbed through the tailor's tongue, a spoon knocked out a tooth, and a knife ran up his thumb.

"And they are dangerous too," said the tailor, dabbing his tongue. And after all, he thought, this is the tongue that says all those important things to the chief people of the land.

But all his customers came because the tailor was a very good tailor, not because he was clever and witty beyond all.

"You should stick to your fine seams," said his cat. "That is your skill."

"I do not know that," said the tailor. "Perhaps I shall lay down my needle and become the Member for Parliament."

He thought about this, and he thought about that, and what the world might give him, and in a few days he looked about the house and said, "What is more, this scratched furniture will have to go. I cannot have this shabby deal and ancient elm and rugged oak, covered with dust. What will they think when they come" – and he was sure they would – "if I do not have inlaid mahogany?"

And a grieving chair that had served a hundred years, broke under him and tipped him and the cat on the floor. It was not the furniture's fault that it was dusty.

"You are growing far too fat," the tailor told the cat. "See what has happened, and think what the Lord Chamberlain might say if my chair tipped him on the floor like that. I am quite disgraced."

So it was no wonder that these things no longer served him well. Never a dab of polish did he put on, never a lick of the duster or a stroke of the broom. All his care was for his needles and his chalk and his tape, and more still for the regard of the high and mighty. He thought he might became one of them by using his tongue. He had a lucky tongue, but not a shining mind.

And then the house itself was found to be at fault, with its plain and tired timbers all across its front. "It should be new and made of stone," the tailor said. "My customers will be ashamed to call."

So then the chimneys smoked, and down came plaster from the ceilings and rain dripped through the roof.

"It's not worth catching mice in these circumstances," said the cat.

"I deserve much better than everything I've got," said the tailor. "As for that cat of mine, I do not like its colourway."

Then in his shop he sat and sewed, and learned judges came and heard him speak and took away his words and laughed at him.

But in his house they did not laugh. They were no longer good enough for him, and thought that they should leave.

"We'll find another home," the worn-down silver forks and knives and spoons declared. "We'll set up on our own."

"We have our legs," the furniture proclaimed. "We'll go where we like, and when we like. We'll not stay to be insulted."

"It will be painful rooting up the cellar," said the house itself. "But I shall try. I shall be free-standing and detached and in a garden of my own."

That very afternoon, when the tailor sat cross-legged upon a stool in his shop, the knives and forks climbed down from where they lay. Their leader was a wooden and experienced spoon.

"We'll go straight out," he said, "and line up in the street. Beware of dogs and children; do not speak to strange utensils."

"We shall follow," said the furniture, led by a grave majestic wardrobe full of tailored clothes.

"I shall come last," said the house. "My attic will advise me where to situate and put foundations down, and my rateable value."

"But do not bring the tailor," said the rest of the goods.

The cutlery rose sharply up, cut through the cupboard door, and led the way into the street.

After them the chairs walked out and sat themselves

along the pavement, with following them a shy and drop-leaf table, a corner cupboard, a piano, the dresser, a *chaise-longue*, oh, and the lot. The scuttle full of coal spilt all its good Welsh nuts, and the longcase clock struck twenty-three.

Last of all the house pulled up its cellar and its drains, and followed out, complete with carpets.

Along the street they went all in a dance and chivaree until they found an empty place.

"Hurrah, hurrah," they shouted, and from the other houses of the street came little things that longed to be away; there was a corkscrew, and a toffee-hammer, and a book of sermons by a Reverend Dean; there were garden shears and tired tablecloths and four whole chandeliers.

"We've left the tailor," said the knives and forks. "We shall set up a commune and do just what we like and wash only when we need, if then."

"Just let me settle in," said the house, and dug himself a place for cellar and for scullery, and laid his drains to rest. "I like my new address. Perhaps I shall be married in the end and be double-fronted, or grow bay windows and some steps. Or bear a doll's house and buy some children for it to play with."

The furniture made itself at home at once. It knew where it had always wished to stand and now it made its choice. "The view, the view," it said. "No longer back to the window all the time."

Last of all the cutlery and the plates and other kitchen stuff found their best places and arranged themselves.

Only the tailor still sat in his shop cross-legged stitching while the city merchants heard his words and had their garments fitted.

"Where is your house and all your gear?" they asked him.

"Oh," said he, "they've gone on their annual holiday beside the sea. There's just me and my needle left. And of course I have the cat."

But that was beyond the truth he knew, because the cat had followed where the house had gone and walked in at the door. "I do not mind where I am," said the cat. "So long as it is here."

And the tailor sits and wonders in his little shop, and sleeps upon the ironing board. He is too proud to notice that his house has left him, so nothing can be done.

But he wonders who is partying by day and night a little further down Cheapside, down along a little lane.

In the merchants' offices they talk of the droll sewing man who never hits it right, or only when he stitches.

At the house, now quietly called 17, they have hired a housekeeper to keep them clean and warm and polish all the silver till she can see through it.

✂ *How to See Them* ✂

Sukey Limner was an old midwife out in the District somewhere, and she'd attended hundreds of mothers and their new babies in her time, along with the young doctors. Some mothers she might have attended, maybe, fifteen times, each time with a new doctor. She brought the young doctors up, she often said, and that's how they knew what to do when they went out in the world.

Sukey retired in the end and got her pension, and she and her husband Jack lived on in peace.

But one day, and it was a foggy evening, a smoggy night, you couldn't see to cough, but Sukey was born and bred herself to these pavements, and Jack wanted an extra relish to his supper.

Sukey found her way well enough through the fog to the shop and got a jar of pickled onions.

She was on her way home with them, and somewhere between two lamp posts, the darkest bit, she felt one and another tugging at her skirt, like a child.

"Well, son, what is it?" she asked, thinking it was a little boy, and maybe lost.

It was a small man, very small he was, and, well, foggy through, she said after.

"I've been catching up to you," he said, with his little

peaky face. "We need you, missus. I can't a-find my way to the hospital in this murk, and my wife, her time has come."

There was nothing new in this, except the littleness of the man. Even when she retired Sukey got called now and then in an emergency.

All the same she said, "We should be calling the ambulance, and see if they can make it."

"No, no," said the little man. "No time, you come at once. There's no telephones at our hospital."

Sukey thought that was strange, but maybe these were Whole Earth freaks. But she was sure she could come to no harm, so she tucked her pickled onions under her arm, wrapped her shawl more tight round her, and followed.

"I thought I knowed the District better than I knowed how to birth a child," she said later. "But I never found a way back there, and I don't know how I found a way out."

In some tangle of alleys they came to a door, and not a very high one either, and in goes the little fellow.

"Quick," he said, and Sukey bent her head down and came into the room where the mother-to-be was lying.

She had expected some sort of foreigners, immigrants very likely, who don't want to get noticed and sent back. She had a few words of some languages, like Maltese and Chinese.

She saw the mother all wrapped. She thought it was in shawls, but she knew very soon she wouldn't have this language, because the bright things weren't shawls, but wings. This was a fairy birth.

"I never did this before," she told the little man.

"It is all the same," said the little man, taking up a small pot. "But we don't know about it at all. Just one thing

though. When the baby is born, before you wrap it up, put some of this green ointment on its eyes. Then wash and wipe your own hands, for you don't want to see what we folk see. The bowl and the napkin will be on the table."

"If that ointment won't harm the baby," said Sukey. "There's no doctor to sign scripts and no chemist to put them up."

"If it can't see what we see," said the mother, "why then it is as good as blind."

"Then, if I don't do it, you will," said Sukey. "And I have the touch for babies, so I'll oblige."

Anyway, the little fellow was right, that this was just like any new creature being born, and out it came without much trouble, and cried out and it was fairy girl, which both parents were pleased about.

And at the very first, just as they said, it couldn't see them, only Sukey, which it didn't like too much, but they never do.

Its little eyes, though they were open and looking, seemed locked shut and murky, until the ointment cleared them, and then it saw its parents.

It also saw many other things that made it laugh, and reached up its new-born hands to play with them.

That's a very forward sort of little girl, thought Sukey.

Then, her work done, the two little parents began to fade

from Sukey's sight.

She felt two gold coins going into her hand, and there she was standing in the little room, and the little door open behind her, and on a table the bowl and a napkin, which she had been told about.

And there, on the corner of her medicine finger, the ring-finger of her left hand, which she had used, was still a trace of the green ointment.

"I'd be able to see that," said Sukey to herself, and up with that finger to her own left eye, and there it stung a little, and there it soothed, and then that eye saw what no eye saw before, how the world was full of another set of people, little flying things, sweet and lovely, and those walking, and other houses and a different city nothing like the grimy District.

Then Sukey washed her hands, and wiped them, and went out of the door into the fog.

She didn't know which place she was in, so she had to close her left eye or be dazzled. And the right eye was full of fog. And when she remembered her jar of pickled onions she could not go back for them, because the little doorway had gone and only a brick wall was left, with either eye.

But she got home well enough, and Jack grumbled and did without onions.

But from that time on Sukey was bothered by her left eye if she kept it open. And then she was bothered by her right eye if she kept that open. She could work along with either of them, in two different worlds.

Only, her own world began to seem dismal and dirty, and the other world she could never belong to, only see.

She had the worst of both, and began to wonder how to get better of herself.

Then one day in the market a speck of dust flew into her right eye, and she had to use the left one. In front of her she saw the little man again, with his pointed face.

"Now, Sukey," he said, "how are you getting on?"

"This way and that," said Sukey, feeling a bit guilty.

"But you can see and hear me," said the little man. "So that means you touched your eye with that ointment, just as I told you not to do."

"It has been no good to me," said Sukey. "You should have said more than you did."

"I said enough," said the little man. "And I paid you in spite of that. Now what do you want?"

"I want the ointment against the first one," said Sukey, "and be rid of your bothersome land."

The little man told her to go with him, and maybe there was something to be done at their hospital.

Sukey trusted hospitals, enough to get on with, not expecting too much or hoping too little. So she followed. They came to a place she never saw before, and inside to the fairy operating room, and fairy doctor.

He looked at her and rustled his wings. "We can stop that eye seeing wrong," he said. And then he put his hand up, and with a sort of twist and a pull, like chewing gum snapping free, Sukey thought, he had the eye in his hand.

"But you've took it," said Sukey. "I didn't mean that."

"I've took it out," said the fairy doctor. "You can have it back. Just keep it carefully if you ever want to use it. Best kept in vinegar, I'd say."

And the first little man says, "You left your pickled onions when you came that night, but we kept them by and here they are."

"And just room in the vinegar for that eye," said the doctor.

And the eye went in, so you could hardly tell which was which. But it was a devil for looking.

Sukey found herself back in the market again, with her jar. She could see again with just the one eye, and it all looked better. But she felt strange, all the same, and went home to get Jack his dinner, and had a lie-down herself.

When she came down to give Jack his tea, "I never had pickled onions like them," he said. "There was one in particular the best I ever tasted. See we always get that brand again, Sukey."

Of course, there were just onions in the vinegar by then. And Sukey never said a word, so how do you know about it?

The End